There, In The Doorway, Stood Chad.

He smiled across the room at his stunned ex-wife and said, "May I come inside out of the rain?"

How like him to intrude back into her life this way! Jo couldn't form a single word; she was in shock.

He smiled as a man does whose life is beyond his control. "I've taken a leave of absence and moved up here."

In stark horror, Jo uttered a guttural, "No!"

"If it's okay with you, I'll leave these wet things down here tonight. Are we roomies?"

"No!" she gasped. But Chad clearly had other ideas....

Dear Reader,

Go no further! I want you to read all about what's in store for you this month at Silhouette Desire. First, there's the moment you've all been waiting for, the triumphant return of Joan Hohl's BIG BAD WOLFE series! MAN OF THE MONTH Cameron Wolfe "stars" in the absolutely wonderful *Wolfe Wedding*. This book, Joan's twenty-fifth Silhouette title, is a keeper. So if you plan on giving it to someone to read I suggest you get one for yourself *and* one for a friend—it's that good!

In addition, it's always exciting for me to present a unique new miniseries, and SONS AND LOVERS is just such a series. Lucas, Ridge and Reese are all brothers with a secret past... and a romantic future. The series begins with *Lucas: The Loner* by Cindy Gerard, and continues in February with *Reese: The Untamed* by Susan Connell and in March with *Ridge: The Avenger* by Leanne Banks. Don't miss them!

If you like humor, don't miss *Peachy's Proposal*, the next book in Carole Buck's charming, fun-filled WEDDING BELLES series, or *My House or Yours?* the latest from Lass Small.

If ranches are a place you'd like to visit, you must check out Barbara McMahon's *Cowboy's Bride*. And this month is completed with a dramatic, sensuous love story from Metsy Hingle. The story is called *Surrender,* and I think you'll surrender to the talents of this wonderful new writer.

Sincerely,

Lucia Macro
Senior Editor

Please address questions and book requests to:
Silhouette Reader Service
U.S.: 3010 Walden Ave., P.O. Box 1325, Buffalo, NY 14269
Canadian: P.O. Box 609, Fort Erie, Ont. L2A 5X3

Lass Small
MY HOUSE OR YOURS?

SILHOUETTE *Desire*®
Published by Silhouette Books
America's Publisher of Contemporary Romance

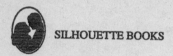

SILHOUETTE BOOKS

ISBN 0-373-05974-4

MY HOUSE OR YOURS?

Copyright © 1996 by Lass Small

This edition published by arrangement with Harlequin Books S.A.

® and TM are trademarks of Harlequin Books S.A., used under license. Trademarks indicated with ® are registered in the United States Patent and Trademark Office, the Canadian Trade Marks Office and in other countries.

Printed in U.S.A.

Books by Lass Small

LASS SMALL

finds living on this planet at this time a fascinating experience. People are amazing. She thinks that to be a teller of tales of people, places and things is absolutely marvelous. This is Lass's 40th book for Silhouette!

To my new editor, Marcia Book Adirim,
a.k.a. "Mab."

One

That late-January day, the Dallas-Fort Worth airport was jammed. The weather there was TEXAS weather and marvelous, as usual. But north of TEXAS just about all the airports clear across most of the United States were closed because of The Storm.

In the complex, where one pack of delayed passengers stood, there was the under-sound of people moving and talking and complaining. It was like a muted roar. Here and there a single voice surfaced and like a fish leaping from turbulent waters can be seen, the sound of restless people could be heard.

The question was asked by one of the ski people, "Did you hear anything about Colorado?"

Across heads, the replying voice was sour with the reply. "Snowed under."

Another voice then inquired, "Well, what do you expect this time of year?"

There's always someone logical who is exceptionally distasteful to be around at a time like that.

From a relentless optimist, there was the comment, "When you get to the slopes, there'll be just that much more snow!"

A good attitude.

Then a male voice called over the packed heads, "How's Chicago? I can't see the board from here."

A female who was closer to the board complained crossly, "Socked in."

Some clown commented in surprise, "They ski in Chicago?"

And from farther back in the crowd, a voice said crossly, "I didn't take time off work in order to sleep on a chair or on the floor in an airport."

Since Jo Morris was a seasoned air traveler, she was not perturbed. With her brown eyes, she was a cool, collected, twenty-eight-year-old. She was a flexible woman who could handle any unexpected situation. Well, most.

She was a program problem-solver for one of the awesome computer greats. She really knew computers. She'd been on the first wave at fourteen with an Apple II Plus.

"Attention, please." The voice was wonderfully male. It was the *Do Not Fear. I Am In Control*-type voice. He was at one of the flight counters. He had all their attentions.

He was a marvelous-looking, well-made man in a perfect uniform who was asking the muttering crowd to listen to him. He'd had all the female attention right away.

No one in the trapped pack believed there was any solution. They were mostly restless and disappointed, and some were sulky, but they all quieted down.

It was unarguable that the airport had no control over the weather that was lousing up other airports someplace else. Or even if by some miracle bad weather sneaked into TEXAS, who could control weather? So why would anyone be angry with the airport personnel?

The person addressing them was a captain of one of the stranded planes. He stood on a movable step-up and scanned the crowd. As always happened when men scanned crowds, and Jo was in the crowd, the man's eyes landed on her. He smiled in the way men smile at a woman who interests them.

And it was mostly to Jo that he said, "I have some hotel rooms available. Because of the locations in the hotels, they are not choice rooms, but you can shower and rest. It would be better if you could double up." He smiled at Jo. "It would be rude to use a double room as a single. Who's double? Raise your hands."

A man's voice next to Jo said, "We are."

While she was recovering from the sound of him, a slip of paper was passed from the pilot to the hand that reached past Jo's shoulder.

In the crush, a body pressed slightly against Jo's side. And her own body reacted strongly. That was weird. She hadn't reacted to any touches since—

"Well, Jo," a nicely rumbling voice said in her ear. "Want to share . . . again?"

All the bedlam around faded away as she turned like a particle in a slowly melting glacier. She didn't have to turn far, but it took a long time and her lips parted during the same millennium.

Since a millennium takes a while to pass, she had the time to notice, in all that while, no one around aged. Interesting. They were all locked in by her shock, but they appeared unaware of what had happened.

Eventually her slight, slow turn did take her stare to the speaker at her shoulder. And it was, indeed, he. Her ex-husband.

He looked the same. His brown hair was thick. His brown eyes were lazy and amused. He was thirty-eight and old enough not to accost an ex-wife.

She spoke. She said, "Chad." With him, she'd always been a similarly brilliant conversationalist. She hadn't actually needed to talk, but her inability to communicate was why she had her master's degree. It was one of the reasons.

He smiled at her as if they'd amicably parted just last week. "So you do remember."

"How amazing to run into you here." Not having seen him in so long, she could evaluate him more critically.

He looked fantastic. No wonder all the female students in his seminars stared and shifted in their chairs. Just seeing him, her own body was being crass. At twenty-eight, she was old enough to have better control.

He lifted the paper slip to call her attention to it. "I have a room. You're my first choice. Want to share?"

How could her body carry on that way? Did it expect— Of course not. Then why— Her mouth said, "Why, how amazing to run into you in an airport!" And she was immediately aware she'd already said something similar. In turn, he would immediately know he'd boggled her.

He always had.

Females acted so silly around Chad Wilkins that he'd accepted it as the normal behavior pattern in women. He simply assumed all women, at all times, acted the way she did around him. He used her conduct as a measuring stick for women. He had never assimilated his lure and he wasn't at all egotistical about himself.

He'd never been very bright about women.

In the crush, the stranded pilot had come through the mob, and he touched Jo's shoulder. "Are you alone? There's one vacant room left. It's mine." His grin was just great.

Why couldn't she just go along with the pilot? It was the perfect escape from Chad. She could make an excuse later with the pilot. But she should seize on this chance to avoid the temptation and escape Chad!

However, Chad smiled kindly at the discreetly salivating pilot and replied, "She's with me."

That had a familiar ring to it. And Jo remembered Chad saying that to friendly men. But then after he'd shooed off whomever, he would tilt his head down to listen to some foggy old man's dissertation on something so obscure as to be beyond heeding.

The pilot, who wasn't empty peanut shells, gave Chad a studying look, then returned his regard to Jo. "If it doesn't pan out, I'm in 409."

She looked at him in serious regret. There stood a normal man. And she heard as her mouth said, "Thank you. But don't wait up."

The pilot waited for more.

She again looked at him regretfully, but she slowly turned back to Chad, taking another millennium to do that simple thing.

Her ex-husband ignored the reluctant-to-give-up pilot who'd never before been turned down. Chad took hold of Jo's elbow as if she was property. Come to think of it, he'd always been possessive.

Chad asked Jo, "Where are your things?"

"Here." She indicated the across-her-body, shoulder-slung, light bag. "I travel light."

He accepted that as logical and informed her with confidence, "I'll find a cab."

And he would. He always could. In all the time Jo had known Chad, he could solve anything. But not Jo. He had never been able to solve Jo.

As they plowed through the packed people, the divorced pair left the abandoned pilot watching after them.

Chad got the first cab that was available. Of course he would. He invited any of the waiting others who were going to that particular hotel to join them. Altogether, not counting the driver, they squeezed in six.

"This many's illegal." The woman driver mentioned her evaluation—to Chad. She would sort him out as their leader.

With authority, Chad gently instructed the cabdriver, "It's an emergency." With a pithy, deliberate pause, he added, "And we tip well."

That was language the driver understood. Most people recognized Chad's position as unheralded leader right away. The cabdriver was no exception. Males sometimes had trouble with the premise of Chad's superiority, as had the pilot, but most people finally would accept the fact that Chad was the leader.

Leaders have very little spare time.

In the cab, Jo was squashed between Chad and the window. He had arranged it so that no other man was close to her. He'd been deft about it. He'd always done that. He could shift her quite discreetly from one side of him to the other depending on who was crowding her.

He was possessive.

Not anymore. They'd been divorced for almost four years. He'd allowed her to leave quite thoughtfully. He'd said, *You'll be back when you've had a taste of being on your own for a while. You like being married!*

He'd been wrong.

It was probably the only time, in all the while she'd known Chad, that he'd ever been wrong. Well, any person was entitled to one mistake in his life.

She had been his.

Sitting forward in the cab on the edge of the back seat, with Chad pressed against her hip and the noisy shadows of other people packed in the small enclosure, Jo's body was afire with ants of desire. How foolish of her sex to react again and so violently to Chad.

She was going to be circumspect and aloof. She was going to show Chad that she did not miss him. That she did not want to be married to him again. And that she was free.

So... he'd been good in bed. She remembered that. Her body remembered it, too. She acknowledged it. She was not really susceptible to Chad. *She was not!*

There were undoubtedly other men who could do sex as well as Chad Wilkins. All men had the same equipment, and it was traditionally done in various ways that were pleasurable to women. And—

He'd been really, *really* good at it.

But that was all. And it was only sex, after all. He had not been a companion or a friend or a helpmate.

He'd been good in bed...on the floor...against the wall. She could admit that, but otherwise he'd been gone.

There were all those meetings with students in his department, meetings with lagging students, meetings with those who were exceptional and those engrossed in projects. There were faculty meetings, the faculty senate and other occasions that were formal, which had included the wives.

Chad had never been around when she had needed him. Of course, her problem was that it had only been his companionship she had wanted. It hadn't been as important to him. Just being together and talking, or not, hadn't been urgent. It could be postponed. Forever.

They'd reached the hotel. She got out first, and it was familiar to wait as he settled up the fares and tips. With the tips given, the cabdriver probably quit for the day.

The January weather in Fort Worth was glorious. It was warm. The TEXAS sun was assuringly benevolent, showing the non-TEXANs that the world could indeed be perfect. The ski equipped, reluctant guests were beginning to perk up and look around for entertainment. They would have a stimulating time and probably end up swimming outside.

Among the stranded strangers, there was the couple who was meeting for the first time since their divorce. So. It was no big deal. They were as ships which pass on the ocean. They would pass with a courteous greeting and some pleasant conversation and . . . separate . . . to go their ways?

He probably had papers to read. He always had a student who needed extra help. Jo hadn't needed anything. She'd never had any problems. So she'd needed no special attention from her husband.

Or so he had thought.

His meals had been on time . . . or held . . . or stored away. The house was always clean. His shirts were pristine and the buttons were all sewn on. His clothes came back from the cleaner on time.

She'd slept in his bed and had been available. Hungrily available. She'd sought him. His laugh had been so intimate. So pleased. His sounds were so basic.

He had been a superior lover. It was quite probable that he still was.

Jo wondered who . . . who all had been sharing his bed. He wouldn't even have to ask. He'd probably have to post a list for day and time. It was a wonder he looked so well, so cared for. Who was taking care of him now? He looked so rested.

Of course, he'd been away from campus. He'd been to a seminar to read a paper. No, not a newspaper. One of his. On . . . what all. Some subject that was so dim and distant that few others would find it interesting. He was such a niggler. He was the type whose concentration was intense. He sorted and sought and paced as he thought.

In her ear, he said, "Let me carry that."

She lifted her brows in question.

"Your bag."

She replied in a dismissing manner, "It's quite comfortable, and I'm used to it. No problem."

He was serious and his lower lip was being obvious. "It seems crass for you to have to carry your things."

She slid her eyes over to give him a narrow, sophisticated understanding of his wiles, but he was frowning at her bag. "When did you get so thin? Are you okay?"

"I've lost five pounds since our divorce almost four years ago."

He flinched. "Don't say the word. I've rejected it."

Jo lowered her eyelids and looked at him with some snide understanding. "Just recently?"

He replied like a stubborn man who hasn't adjusted to reality. "No. Ever since you walked out on me."

They'd stopped at the hotel's desk to register. He said to her, "Wait here."

She told him firmly, "I need to pay half."

"No."

She replied in an adult manner, "I have a credit card for my expense account."

"No."

Come to think of it, he'd always been that way. His way. That's what was wrong with him, everything had to be his way. Even when he was being darling, he wanted it his way.

Jo said with her being-patient-with-a-client voice, "I pay half or I walk."

"You've become a prostitute?"

She gasped in indignation.

"You were always terrific and so body-hungry that it doesn't surprise me at all. I've spent a lot of time wondering who you were savoring."

Through her teeth she spaced the three words. "I have not!"

He frowned at her and appeared censoring. "Then I feel sorry for the men around you. What do they do?"

Somewhat prissily, she retorted, "Not all men are like you, thank goodness."

He put on an instant lecturing facade. "Goodness has nothing—"

"Be quiet!"

He grinned from ear to ear and said, "There's my Jo. I thought I'd lost her, you've been so polite."

She'd been rude? She frowned and considered. "When haven't I been polite?"

"I haven't had tabs on you in much too long," he informed her as if she hadn't realized such a simple fact. "Do you know I dream about you? Hot dreams." He scowled at her. "Are you living with somebody else?"

"Why do you ask?"

"Well, I'd hate for some irritated guy to come bursting into our room and act upset."

Her "lover" would...act...upset if he found her with another man? "Is that how you would have been? If I'd had an affair, would you have been...upset?"

Mildly he replied, "I'd have ripped out his jugular vein, unkindly."

"Is there a *kind* way?" She looked at him in shock.

"Not where you're concerned."

She was indignant. "We're divorced!"

"I've missed you."

Exasperated, she demanded, "When did you have the time to notice I was gone? How long was it before you realized I wasn't around anymore? You ran out of dishes or shirts? What caught your attention?"

"Every damned empty day." He looked up from the registry and added, "Every lousy, empty night."

"It's been almost four years."

"It's not yet four but it seems like twenty-five."

"I don't believe this."

And he had the gall to inquire, "Why haven't you found another husband?"

"How do you know I haven't?"

"No ring."

Along with supercilious eyebrows, she lifted her hand. "I always remove it when I travel. Don't you?"

He went back to filling out the hotel information. But he said, "I've looked around, but nobody else is you."

His eyes were on the page he was filling out. He had marvelous eyelashes. She couldn't believe he'd actually said the words, that, instead, she'd heard what she wanted him to say.

He finished writing and handed the page to the person at the registration desk. "Two keys."

"Yes, sir." And she handed him the keys.

He picked up his bags and said, "I talk to your father and he has told me you are not married."

"Mistakenly told you? I wonder why he lied. He probably felt you would be upset."

"I'm never upset." Chad was firm. "I can handle most things. You being away so long has bothered me."

"It's taken you almost four years to notice? You probably saw me in the air terminal and thought I looked familiar. Then you'd searched your mind as to which of your classes I'd been in. And finding I wasn't a student, you sorted me out."

"Come back to Indy with me." He punched the button for the elevator. Then he stood and looked at her as the elevator doors opened. He followed her inside the cage and punched the button for the sixth floor. No one else was right there, so the doors closed. They were alone in the elevator.

"Why should I go home with you? You didn't want me. Why should you care about someone else wanting me?"

"I love you."

That ticked her off. "You really irritate me. No wonder I left you. How could you possibly—"

She stopped speaking as the elevator came to a quiet stop. The doors slid open silently. The hall's carpet was discreet and elegant. It was nicely insulated and therefore silent.

On the wall opposite the elevator, they saw the numbers that indicated they were to go to the left. The room was right there. That's why it was still available. It was next to the elevator shaft.

Guests would gather by the elevator and talk. Their voices would be heard in the room. Baggage carts were rolled from the elevator. They too would be heard, even though it was a discreet hotel. So the rooms closest to the elevator were used only in necessity.

Jo got out her key card and put it into the door's lock. She was immediately aware her action startled Chad. He had always opened the doors. She'd usurped his move.

He kept her from entering by dropping his luggage in the hall. One bag clunked heavily. And he bent and picked her up!

"What—?"

He explained casually, "We're going to sleep together. I always carry women into hotel rooms when I intend on sleeping with them."

She gasped indignantly. "Just how many—"

But he kissed her quite skillfully and set the maulable mass that was Josephine Morris over out of the way. He then retrieved his abandoned luggage with perfect coordination.

How had he managed to be functional after that kiss?

How vulgar he was. He had to be very easy with the act of seduction—the preliminaries and the actual act. He planned to...sleep...with her. And he always kissed the women he slept with in hotel rooms.

She inquired with casual coolness, "What's your score total so far?"

"I'll check it out and let you know. The figures aren't at my fingertips this minute. I'll have to consult my computer files."

That sobered her considerably. Chad hadn't missed her at all. He'd been keeping statistics on other women, all of whom he'd carried through hotel room doors and seduced on the beds there.

Jo was crushed. No wonder he'd never contacted her. He hadn't had the time to remember her. How had he even remembered who she was at the airport? He must have caught a glimpse of her and known he'd seen her...somewhere.

Think of having to sort through a wheatfield of women to discover which one she'd been!

He'd probably had to go to the airport's computer base to contact his home computer bank and search out which one she was.

She said, "If you've been traveling much, you must be exhausted."

Chad replied leisurely, "I'm rested up. The seminar was only men and they didn't even mention sex."

"So you're ravenous, and you saw me and remembered me?"

"I assumed I'd had you somewhere along the way, and therefore I was cautious until I validated who you actually are." He watched her with his eyes half-closed. "How many men have you driven wild since you last did that with me?"

She gasped like a virgin accused of dropping a swimsuit shoulder strap.

She moved inside her body in various ways. She was indignant. She moved her lips and she finally said, "Baloney!" And with the word, she could have just died of embarrassment. She might just as well have said, Golly! or something else equally juvenile.

She grabbed up her bag and started for the door.

He caught her arm. "Don't be such a chicken." His voice was so soft, so husky and sweet. His eyes were earnest; his big hand was gentle. He looked soberly into her eyes. She saw as the depths warmed and his crinkles deepened. He had the best mouth.

Since her eyes went to his mouth, he needed to show her why people have mouths, and he kissed her a completely unfair, remarkably sweet, loving kiss. He was really, really good. He really kissed her.

He did.

As he lifted his mouth with all those marvelous little sounds in that silent room, she raised weighty eyelids to look up at him. With some effort she coordinated her vocal cords as her kiss-swollen lips said, "Let's go swim."

He regarded her soberly for some time, then his smile started and his eyes twinkled. He replied, "Right."

He went down to the hotel necessity shop, which sold all sorts of important things like condoms and swimsuits and candy and flowers. They didn't miss a trick.

Jo was in the pool when Chad came out in his swim trunks. He looked like an American Greek god. He was actually Dutch and Welsh with a touch of Irish thrown in.

He dived into the pool effortlessly and his strokes were lazy and strong. He came to her and said, "Take a breath."

She remembered that, and she vigorously back-pedaled away from him. He laughed and swam, following her so easily. He was so at home in the water.

A surprising number of people don't believe in swimming in the winter. Pools are generally closed. Yankees are unpredictable. The weather in TEXAS was so nice that it seemed like a Yankee summer day. The two paying guests played together like otters. They lifted themselves from the pool and went down the slide and they used the pool.

Underwater, he touched her here and there. He lifted her and threw her and made her laugh. Men's muscles are just different. Their strength is awesome. He had no trouble following her in the water, turning her, lifting her. It was easy for him.

He laughed as she splashed him and wiggled and slid away. He could have held her, but if he had, he might have hurt her. He was stronger and had to be careful.

He finally captured her and took her under the water to kiss her.

In all that while, he gave her his entire attention.

How unkind of him.

It was like the time of their courtship, all those years ago, when she was new on campus and he was an assistant professor. But she became his wife. She was a woman of principles and would not go to bed with him without being married to him.

Since she had been married to one of the teaching staff, her schooling was free. She graduated with a degree in business and had taken her masters in business.

When she left him, he had asked if she didn't want to stay on a little longer and earn her doctorate also. He hadn't felt she'd used him. He was practical.

She hadn't used Chad to get her education. It had been boredom that had urged her to take classes. She hadn't gotten pregnant, although they'd used no barriers. Each month had been a disappointment, another failure, before she'd sadly accepted that she was barren.

While she had had his sexual attention, she hadn't had his companionship. She'd been so lonely. She'd wanted his attention. He wasn't around. He would never be around. Eventually, she had understood that and she had left.

So almost four years after their divorce, Jo played as she'd dreamed of playing with Chad all those years ago. At eighteen, at twenty, but at twenty-two the hope had dimmed. During the time she'd been working on her masters, she knew their marriage was doomed.

No miracle happened.

By then, she had faced reality. Her time with Chad would never be any different than it was then.

Looking at Chad soberly, she decided that she might just as well have one last fling with him. Their marriage was water lost over the dam. Why not enjoy the last of the trickle of her time with him? So she laughed, and flung herself into the water and allowed him to chase her.

Their time then was as she'd always thought their marriage could be.

And he took her back to their room. She was breathless from swimming, or something, and she was shy.

"How many men have you had by now?" Chad teased Jo as he dried his hair with a big towel. His eyes were confident. He asked, "Do you have notches on your bedposts?" He paused. "Add notches for these days with me." Then his voice was smokily gruff as he told her, "Put my marks on top of the others."

There were no notches. There had been no other man. She still hadn't gotten over her love for Chad. She hadn't even been tempted to try another man.

But she was ready for Chad.

She met him halfway and she loved him.

He had the newly purchased condoms and he was careful of her as he'd always been. He was gentle and kind with his ravening hunger for her. He controlled himself, but his breaths were harsh and his low moans were exquisitely thrilling. He loved her as he always had.

And it was not enough.

They had a night of love. Her hair was like dried-out, raveled rope. So was his. Her body was well used. So was his.

She was limp and contented. She had forgotten the pleasure, the ecstasy, the thrill of being with him, of being part of him, of making love with him.

And he groaned, "Why did you leave me?"

Tears welled in her eyes. "You were never there."

Agonized, he protested earnestly, "I slept with you every night."

"But the days were long and empty."

"People live all their lives with other people and see them seldom. Why did you need to be with me all the time?"

"I loved you."

He frowned at her. "To need constant attention like that isn't healthy."

"Probably not." She looked down at the sheet as she drew it up over her. She felt isolated. Just thinking of it all chilled her. It was past. How could she still be affected by those sad, empty times?

TWO

Dallas and Fort Worth are separate big cities and different from one another. Dallas is glitzy and elegant while Fort Worth keeps an iron lock on being Western. There was a time when Fort Worth had been the gathering center for shipping cattle by train. Trucks had changed that.

The building of the shared airport had been a fascinating merger for the cities. Their sprawling populations were reaching out to occupy the area between the cities, and the shared airport was the obvious solution. It had not been easy for Dallas to share it with a "lesser" neighbor who was deliberately lacking in elegance.

Necessity makes for strange bedfellows.

Just as did the meeting between Jo and Chad.

Jo would look at Chad eating breakfast across the

table in their room and she was stunned that she was
with him again.

What were the chances of running into someone
known in an airport? Actually, it wasn't *that* un-
usual. But an ex-husband?

Incredible.

Of course, if one was a film star or multimarried
perhaps, but Jo Morris? Ridiculous.

Chad was in the shower when Jo was startled by the
discreet knock on their door. A knock? Who could
possibly know they were there?

In their shared room, only one bed was rumpled and
askew.

But hotels no longer had house detectives who
checked on morals.

She squinted at her traveling clock and it was only
seven-thirty. Jo inquired as to who was there. With the
reply that it was breakfast, she put on her raincoat
before she opened the door.

The discreet waiter didn't even gasp at her disha-
bille. He conducted himself as if every person in the
hotel was barefooted and wearing a raincoat in their
room. She'd obviously been in some sort of rain because her hair was a tangled mess.

He said not a word but went straight to his work. He
set the small table adroitly and with some skilled
flourish.

She gave him a guilty-conscience tip.

He grinned as he thanked her.

She did not make eye contact. Her glances darted
around and she blushed scarlet. But she was serious-
faced and silent.

With the size of the tip, he felt he had to tidy up a bit. And he moved chairs, retrieved and plumped night-discarded pillows. Did he emphasize that chore?

Jo moved her hands and said, "Never mind."

The waiter grinned big and friendly before he reluctantly left.

She knew full well that the waiter thought she was a loose and easy woman. She was there in one of the giveaway rooms that cost outrageously but less than the others. And she'd come from the overloaded airport with a stranger. *HARLOT* must be written across her forehead in purple on the red blush that suffused her entire face.

Closing the door again, Jo scowled at the torn-up bed with its plumped pillows. Two of the pillows had been taken from the floor. Just as they had some years ago. She and Chad had shared one pillow. That was a clue right there. Then too, the other bed hadn't been touched. How obvious.

There is nothing like a guilty conscience to rattle a seemingly free woman.

She straightened. She would never see the waiter again. She would leave this place. She would go back to her life and this would be a forgotten incident.

Chad came out of the bathroom, gloriously naked, drying his hair with a rough towel. He grinned at her and said, "I'm clean. Let's roll around so that I can smell you instead of just me."

She looked back at him in appalled shock.

He noted she was wearing a raincoat, over nothing, and he lifted his eyebrows a trifle as he smiled. "It's raining inside?"

"That could be what the waiter thought."

He then noted the set table. He said, "Great. We can eat first."

She replied stiffly. "I believe I shall shower."

"No. Don't. You have such a wonderful woman smell."

"I . . . smell?"

And he made savoring sounds as he tried to hold her. He rooted his nose around her throat and tried to loosen the tightly tied coat belt. He inquired, "Going out?"

"I had to put something on to open the door."

"Good thinking."

"He thinks I'm a harlot."

Chad lifted his head back and looked at her. "He said that?"

"No. He smiled in that way."

"What way?"

"As if he knew what we'd been doing."

Chad looked at the one messed-up bed and then he looked back at his ex-wife. "A logical conclusion. The pillows are back where they belong."

"He did that."

Chad tried not to grin too widely. "Tonight we'll mess up the other bed first."

"I am embarrassed."

He was surprised by her. "We're married!"

"We are not. We are divorced!"

"Ah, that doesn't mean anything to a couple. It's just a technicality. We're legal."

"I believe you are tilted in your thinking."

He laughed in a good throat chuckle. "You've always tilted me, one way or another. I had to leave the house so that you could get some rest."

"You gave all your attention to the college, you just used my body now and then."

"You're lucky I had the distraction of a commitment to the college, or you would have never gotten out of bed at all!"

She dismissed him. "You say that after I've been gone for four years—"

"Just over three years."

She confronted the stickler and corrected him. "It is almost four. I'm twenty-eight."

He slid a salacious glance down her body. "You've held together quite well."

She leveled a look at him that showed him her adult maturity and tolerance.

She went to her suitcase, removed a pair of slacks and underwear, then chose a blouse.

"We'll swim after we've breakfasted and read the paper."

She looked up at him. She did want to swim. She took out pajamas and went to the bath, ignoring his very earnest protests.

She returned wearing the green silk pajamas for the first time, and was additionally wrapped in a cover-up of dark blue. She had a towel around her head.

He put down the paper and served her breakfast from the insulated pots.

There was hot cereal, fruit, remarkably sinful iced muffins, milk, tea and sugar mints. He had coffee. He hadn't forgotten any of her needs.

She put the fruit on the cereal, butter and jam on the muffins, and she ate every bite.

When she sat back, he put down his paper and smiled. "Feeling better?"

She regarded the husband she had discarded, and she knew this was her chance to use him as she'd always wanted. He would not change, but this was an opportunity to live out her dream of a relationship.

If she could have him now, she could get him out of her system and then go on her way, freed of him. That was what this unexpected opportunity offered.

She smiled at him.

He laughed. He reached over and cupped her chin in his hand as he leaned to kiss her mouth. Then he lifted his head. His eyelashes almost covered his eyes and the crinkles at the corners deepened. "What a miracle to've found you again."

She didn't again say *baloney* to him. She just looked at him critically, searching for his flaws. As she'd always thought, he had no physical flaw. His flaws were limited to that of cohabitation.

Neglect of a chattel.

But he was trapped there, with her, and he had no escape. No other person could take his attention from her. She could wallow in his concentrated regard. Perhaps then he would know what he had missed in their marriage. And this time, it would be he who was abandoned, to stand alone, bereft, on the plain of nothingness.

Was she taking revenge?

She considered that. But she could not see how he could be harmed. He hadn't changed. His marriage to her had not been important to him.

When they were married, he'd had the opportunity to cherish her or even just to include her in his life. He had not. He would not be harmed by an interlude with her.

It was only now that his clever tongue said things about disliking the word "divorce," but his saying it didn't mean anything. He'd had a long, long time to figure her out. And almost four years ago, he'd agreed to an amicable parting.

Her leaving hadn't upset him or saddened him. He had only inquired if she wouldn't like to stay long enough for her to earn her doctorate. At the time, such a polite question had sundered any lingering hope Jo might have had for their marriage.

Jo looked at her ex-husband and he was as she remembered him, as she'd dreamed of him. She watched him smile at her.

And she smiled back.

He laughed softly in his male throat and coaxed, "Come sit on my lap. I've not held a woman on my lap in too long."

Her body got up and just wiggled right on over and sat itself down on his interested lap.

It was, of course, a part of her plan. She would get all of this kind of foolishness out of her system.

His hands were familiar. He found a mole he'd missed. "I'd wondered if you'd be so foolish as to have this removed. I love this mole. It proves you're human."

"Moleless people are inhuman?"

"Most goddesses don't have moles. Only those who are partly human can contrive to have a mole or so. That fools human males and they believe they are dealing with real women instead of magic ones who can get away. How many other men have you lured?"

"Just you."

He hugged her gently to him and groaned. "I've missed you."

"How can you claim you've missed me?"

"I've felt vacant without you."

"Come on, Chad, you were never around enough to even get acquainted with me. What you missed was the handy sex."

"We did it by hand!"

In an adult way, she explained, "I was available."

"You were the most important thing in my life. Are you finished running around being a single woman? Are you ready to come home? It's time you did, you know. There's a limit to what a good husband will tolerate in a flighty woman who wants to try her wings."

Sitting on his lap, she asked, "Do you actually believe I left you in order to be on my own? I was already. I didn't need to physically leave you. You were gone."

"I was always there."

He said that! He actually said it quite as if he thought he'd always been around!

She instructed, "Other men go home to be with their wives and mow their yards and help."

"They do?"

"You never noticed?" She frowned at him.

"When we lived together, you were looking at other men?" In shock, he leaned back so that he could see her face.

"I wanted only to see you! I loved you. I wanted to be around you. You weren't anywhere around. You were always busy."

"I made our living."

She exclaimed, "Twenty-four hours a day?"

"I wasn't gone all the time."

"You were gone most of the time."

"Being a new assistant professor at Butler University is somewhat demanding, of time, if your students are to be taught what they should know."

"A wife has none of the professor's time."

He said, "I slept with you every night."

"You've mentioned that. You said it at the time. Sleeping isn't one of those chatting times when a couple becomes acquainted and learns what the other person thinks or feels."

"I felt around on you all night long, just about."

She agreed, "Here and there."

He looked at her body. "What did I miss? I thought I'd felt around everywhere."

Jo corrected herself, "Now and then."

"You're still peeved."

"No," she replied. "I've adjusted. I'm going to enjoy this hiatus. When we say goodbye this time, we'll do it better."

"How can leaving me be...better?"

"I'll know why it didn't work the first time. Why it's impossible. I won't yearn for you."

Quite soberly, he asked, "Did you? Did you...yearn for me after you'd left?"

She didn't reply but slowly got off his lap. She removed the towel wrapped around her head and slowly began to rub her hair. Finally she said with some irony, "Chad, I yearned for you while I lived with you."

"Why didn't you tell me?"

She stopped and turned her face to him in disbelief. She just looked at him.

"You did tell me."

"Yes."

"I'm sorry, Jo."

"It's past. Let's go swim."

He sat and watched her. "I've missed you so terribly. I knew you were there to come home to. After you left, I dreamed of your sweet face and your voice. I missed your body in my bed. I remembered how it was to make love with you. Did you remember that?"

"Yes."

He was sure. "We had a good marriage."

"You had a good convenience."

He watched her. "I love you."

"Of course. Let's go swim."

He considered her, her mood, and he mentioned, "You just washed your hair."

She shook her head. "It was so stale from being so sweaty that I would have polluted the pool."

"You always were a stickler. There would be no way that you'd pollute a swimming pool." Then he asked slyly, "Why did you sweat that way?"

She tilted up her chin and replied with some verve, "I haven't a clue."

Chad loved it. He laughed in the way men have when they're flirting with a woman who pleases them.

That time there were other people swimming. But they were earnest lappers and took up only one side. On the other side, the two lovers played. He had his hands on her one way or another all the time. She smiled and flirted and taunted him.

They went back to their room to shower and dress, then they went out to investigate the highlights of Old Fort Worth. They saw the old cattle yards, and they checked out the railroad stations and the old saloons.

They had genuine TEXAS barbecue for lunch, but it wasn't. It was meat with a hot sauce. They drank

Pearl Beer and learned to roll the warmed tortillas so that the hot butter wouldn't run out.

And they went to a theatre, which showed the old, early silent cowboy shorts with accompanying piano music.

One short featured a train engine. The heroine was tied to the train rails. She was rescued by the man-covered engine from a set fire that engulfed the forest. The camera people made it appear the heroine took off fifty petticoats so the men could beat out the roaring blaze.

There were other, similar film shorts, and the viewers loved every one. They could read the text out loud and laugh and chat and not bother the reception of the films. It was fun.

While the pair was casually dressed, they were welcomed to a marvelously elite place for dinner. And they talked as they relished perfect food served precisely. The presentation was an art.

When they returned to the hotel, they found a note saying they could make connections for their flights the next day. They should call.

In their room, the ex-marrieds considered each other quite seriously. And they decided they weren't in that much hurry. So they canceled their reservations at the airport.

Chad called the delay to his college, and Jo reported in to her computer firm in Chicago.

Sharing the cost, they rented a car the next day and drove south to Austin. It is the state capitol. There, they snooped around to hear some great blues and country groups. They viewed the Guadalupe River and picnicked there along that wonderful, lazy waterway, which at one point meandered over a lumpy, white rock bed.

They found out why it's said that the sunshine spends the winter in TEXAS. Of course, San Antonio brags that the winter sun stays only in their area.

The divorced couple walked all over downtown Austin and viewed the red granite state capitol building. They noted the TEXAS trees, and the fact that they are different from those in the north.

They saw the hundreds-of-years-old oak some person had tried to kill with chemicals. The tree was saved, they say, by putting crystals around it to counter the poison. A baffling act.

But along with the crystals, the state resource used countering chemicals. The money spent in saving the oak would have planted a hundred other trees.

There is no other vista like that of TEXAS. The visitors lounged and talked and laughed and looked. They then drove on down to San Antonio, and it was just like the features shown on TV. How amazing to see it actually.

And the Alamo.

A visitor's skin still shivers with the intensity of the emotion still locked in that ground.

The travelers went to Fredricksburg and over to Bandera because someone said they should see the towns. And those different places were worth the trip. The two sightseers used up Chad's entire leave. And it was special.

Unfortunately for Jo, their sojourn was exactly the way she'd expected to share time with Chad. How could he be so perfect? How could he not have shared such time with her during the six years they'd been married?

She felt more cheated than before when she'd only hoped for such a companionship. He was so knowledgeable. That was no surprise. She knew he was curious and erudite. But he was so companionable. How dare he be as magical as she'd always wanted? It made her mourn the lost years.

And it made her wary.

He said, "Quit your job and come home."

He said that.

Not only could she just quit her job, which she loved and which kept her very well indeed, but he called his house and him . . . home.

Probably the worst of it all was that she was tempted.

He phoned in to Butler University in Indianapolis, Indiana, and said he was delayed. He was working on a problem. He would explain when he returned. He said his absence would be stimulating to the grad student who assisted him.

And the reply from Butler University was, "Is there any way we can help?"

Chad replied, "Thank you, no. This is a personal problem. I will solve it. But it might take several more days."

"Call us if we can help."

"Thank you." And Chad hung up with a pleased smile.

They drove the rental car on down to Padre Island. There they could wade not only in the Gulf, but in the influx of Winter TEXANS. Before all the druggies, the farmers from the north wintering in TEXAS were called Snow Birds. The snow birds fly south, and so do the idle farmers. Well, actually they don't all fly, they mostly just drive motor homes down. Now the Yankee farmers are called Winter TEXANS and they are included as citizens. Contributing citizens. They help the economy.

Without comment, the two idlers viewed the havoc wrought by intruding entrepreneurs on Padre Island. It was filled with high rise condos and hotels on either side of the sand island. And there were paved double highways down the middle of the sandbar. In all of that south TEXAS land, the buildings were a surprise. The rest of the area wasn't so intruded upon.

The visiting pair drove over into Mexico and went through the shops. They bought wooden toys beautifully colored—tops, flutes and cups to catch an attached ball and yo-yos. They bought rawhide vests that were lined with sheep wool.

Chad bought Jo a designer watch, and a toad purse with a zipper on its stomach.

She was unsure about the zippered toad.

He explained in his class lecturing voice, "It's a prince frog. When you kiss it, it will become a prince. For this metamorphosis, you have to take it to bed with you."

She gave him a careful look.

Chad frowned with false impatience. "Don't you remember the fairy tale?"

She said sober faced, "Yeah. Sure."

"I'll explain when we get home."

He did keep mentioning they would be going "home" to Indiana.

But she knew better. They would part long before that could ever happen.

In Mexico, she bought a dress that was swirly and colorful, and she bought him a white, loose, cotton, beautifully embroidered pullover shirt. With it were slim black trousers.

They bought huaraches, the leather strip woven, flat shoes that are so squeaky and interesting. And comfortable.

She found a blue felt jacket that was embroidered with yarn. It was just right. There were two pockets for her hands. The edges of the sleeves and the jacket were cross-stitched with the yarn of the decorations. It was different.

They returned the short distance to the Rio Grande, crossed back over the river into their own country and drove back to their hotel on Padre Island.

They dressed for supper. They were so companionable and intimate that Jo thought of their marriage. Had they ever had this easy closeness? This comfortable silence?

In all that time, she'd wanted the companionship that was then between them. When had they ever had the time to be silent friends? They'd had just been— silent. Either that or talking about some student who worried Chad. Then the conversation had been his verbal thinking on how to help or alter directions for the troubled one.

At that time, why hadn't she said to Chad, "I'm not oriented. I'm unsure. I need help." She never had. She'd listened. She hadn't even been old enough to have opinions to help. She hadn't had the ideas to contribute. Nor had she known how to discuss her isolation.

He had felt he was sharing.

She had felt left out, left behind, lacking in experience.

So did she now have the experience to help out? To listen? To observe?

Jo looked at her ex-husband. He was miles away. He was thinking about something else altogether. She could not hold his attention, even now.

He caught her observation. He said, "What would you think about coming back to Indiana with me? You are so self-confident now, that I believe you could handle being a prof's wife. Let's see, shall we? I want you back. I've missed you like bloody hell."

"How could anyone miss anything 'like bloody hell' and actually want it? That sounds quite awful."

"That's how it's been for me since you left."

"You've hidden it well."

"I married you too soon. You needed some adult shine—that's like city shine for a country boy."

"You've been researching living with a student?"

"In all this time, I've talked to your dad. He's told me where you are, what you're doing and if you're going with anyone very much. He's kept me in touch."

"You've actually, really been talking to Dad?"

"I like him."

"What all has he said?"

"To be patient. You need to mature."

She gasped in indignation, "He would *never* have told you that!"

Chad nodded and replied, "Actually, he said you're immature. That you take after your mother who took years to become adult."

"He did not say that!"

Chad laughed. "No, he didn't. He's hard-nosed and it took me forever to just get him to recognize that I love you, and I'd wait through anything to get you back.''

"Hah!"

"That 'hah' is proof you haven't made it yet, but it's better than 'baloney' or—''

She shrieked!

He frowned and complained, "Now what am I going to say when all the TEXANS come arunning to defend your honor?"

"You'll think of something smooth. You'll probably say I'm backing out on an agreement to, uh, co-operate."

He smiled and said, "Great! I knew you'd come up with the perfect defense. Thank—"

"I'll tell the truth."

He was disgusted. "You've always been a stickler."

"What did my mother say in all these conversations?"

"She won't speak to me. She thinks I'm a rat."

Jo laughed. "Really? I misjudged her! I thought she'd be on your side."

"What does she say to you?"

"That I'm a fool to let you get away."

He nodded again. "With parents as logical as yours, how did you get the way you are?"

"Dad says I'm not his, and mother claims I'm a throwback."

"Thrown away?"

She enunciated clearly as she finished the sentence, "—of another time."

Three

It was very interesting how Chad could manuever Jo. She was trusting. She was used to computer hacks who were open, honest and sharing. It never really entered her head that Chad was sly.

On their way back north, they did not drive through one single place that had a commercial airport. It was incredible, especially in TEXAS where the distances are far.

Once she said, "I'd no idea the land in TEXAS was so isolated."

And he'd had the gall to reply, "Yeah."

They were going up the west side of the state so that, he said, he could see the "real West" for comparison as to the progress in the rest of the country. That was exactly what Chad told Jo.

Chad would go into a filling station miles from nowhere and come back to say to Jo, "Darn, we passed the turnoff too far back."

Jo would look at the map and hunt. Then she'd look up and ask, "Where is this place on the map?"

And he'd study it and point out a vacant space. "We're here."

She'd study it from all angles while she bit her lip and ruffled her hair as she searched the minute dots in that great blank area. She was so diligent that she'd always find something, and she'd tell Chad, "Here's one. It might just be a double seater, but it could get me to another airport."

With interest, he'd reply, "Let me see. Yeah, but that's out of our way. See? There's a Council Bluff there. It's an Indian meeting place."

The sides of her mouth turned down as she retorted, "It seems to me those Indians did a lot of meeting."

He nodded and agreed, "Probably trying to figure a way to get rid of us."

With some interest, she asked, "Since you teach World History, how did Europeans manage to 'discover' all the virgin lands? I understand there were nine hundred tribes of Indians living just in TEXAS at the time the Spanish landed and 'discovered' this 'uninhabited' country."

"It's attitude," he explained kindly. "It's like your inability to see mice."

She disagreed, "It was the traps I couldn't empty."

"You threw the trap away with the poor little, limp, dead body still trapped and you bought new traps."

She observed, "You're very knowledgeable. I hadn't realized you were aware of that problem. When did you notice?"

"You kept a neat stack of receipts. They were fascinating reading."

She slid a sideways look at him. "You were a snoop."

As he drove along, he moved out his one arm in an entirely open communication of fact with no secrets. "I had to know how our money was being spent so quickly. It was mostly on mousetraps."

Prissily, she retorted, "I bought an occasional lipstick."

"A hussy." He agreed with the label for her.

She tilted back her head and lifted her eyebrows. "I curled my own hair."

He smiled.

She mentioned, "You're a tightwad."

He watched the road kindly. Since he'd lured her attention from the map, he continued his distraction. "In your checking account at home is something close to six thousand dollars, that's with interest, which is the accumulation of your pin money."

"Is that what's paying for this car?"

He licked his smile. "No."

She reminded him, "We are divorced. You have no responsibility toward me. The money is yours."

He corrected her, "We're not divorced, we're just separated. You've had to have room to stretch, and you needed to be away from me to do that because I tend to control." He elaborated in an aside, "The need to control is just part of being a teacher."

"I hadn't noticed control as much as absence."

He chided her, "You sent my checks back."

"For almost six years, you'd paid for my room and board, and it was because of your teaching position that I also have my master's."

He watched the road as he bit his lower lip in thought. "I hadn't thought of it that way. I thought of you as more than a bedmate. If I'd known you were lending me your body in exchange for your education, I'd have felt more— What are you doing? Stop that!" He grabbed her arm as he swerved the car on the isolated road and pulled to a stop. "What the hell's the matter with you?"

With the door half-open, furiously rigid, her eyes shooting sparks, she said at him over her shoulder, "I was your wife!"

"Aw, honey, I know that. I was teasing."

"You lecher!"

"Well, yes. But I'm also your husband." He smiled at the angry woman and soothed. "I was teasing. Honest."

But she started to cry.

He was stunned. With the car stopped, he turned to her, gentled and concerned. "Did I hurt you?"

She gulped and her trembling voice retorted, "For years."

He was silent for a while as she barely allowed him to hold her. Her softness was squashed by the smoothed planes of his male body. He rubbed his chest just a bit against her movable breasts, and he groaned.

Then he said in a rather foggy manner, "I hadn't really understood how young you were." He moved his face around on hers and his breathing became different. His hands were a little careless.

He told her, "You seemed so in control. But now I realize you were very young. Did you latch on to me because I was older and you missed your folks?"

She moved her head back so that he could search her throat with his day's budding whiskers. While she liked being whiskered, she did say, "I did not 'latch' on to you. I was an independent woman . . . until I fell in love with you. That was my mistake."

He reared his head in shock and looked at her as he exclaimed, "Do you think for one minute that loving me was a mistake?"

She wiggled a little to get closer and her hand on the back of his head pulled his whiskering back to her throat. She communicated the fact, "A deadly one. I believe being put on the rack and stretched would have been more kind."

He said the obvious with some indignation, "You told me everything, I didn't need to torture you."

Moving her body so that his hands could grope her more intimately, she accused, "But you ignored me, and that was a greater torture."

As his hands moved on her seductively, he made hungry sounds. He moved the tip of his tongue around in her ear. "I had no idea you were that dependent. I thought of you as being free."

"I love y— I loved you."

He'd heard the change and looked at his ex-wife. His heart smiled as he licked the grin from his own lips and tried to appear as serious as her words indicated the confrontation to be.

So they sat there, she locked in his python wrap, and he comforted her. He talked sweet talk. He'd never done that before.

She asked sulkily, "Who have you been around that you can talk that way? You've never before said those things to me."

His voice so close and low and rumbly, he replied with slow sensuousness, "It must be the TEXAS water. Before now, my conversations have involved only history. Well. Come to think of it, we're getting a history going just for us. We've known each other longer and longer with every day that passes."

Moving her chest and shoulders slightly, she told him, "We haven't seen one another in almost four years and—"

Gently he corrected, "It's just past three."

"Almost four." She countered him yet again. "So there is a gap."

He moved his face down to rub it against her soft breasts, which had somehow lost their covering. But he did respond to her. "It's given us time to evaluate the past. I've missed you. Let's go back to Indy and start over."

She squirmed her body a tad. "That would be foolish." Her knees were restless.

"No. Everyone there will understand."

She almost made it out of the car again. When he'd pinned her so that she couldn't even wiggle, he asked with candid interest, "What set you off that time?"

She accused, "You said that after seeing me again, everyone at Butler will understand."

He was perfectly logical, "They will! They're open-minded and would see that you've gr—" He stopped.

Suspiciously, with narrowed eyes she guessed, "I've . . . grown up? Is that what you're saying? Is it? Are you implying I was juvenile?"

No man in his right mind would *touch* that question. But Chad readily replied, "You're solid."

"I've gained weight?" She regarded him as if he was hornswoggling her. As if he pretended he'd just landed from some remote star.

She was letting him dig his own grave. And he was doing it quite nicely.

With interest, he guessed, "You're mature?"

She snapped in a deadly reply, "I was a skinny adolescent?"

He gave her a sharing grin. "You were the greenest I'd ever encountered."

Pushing a tad more she asked, "Easy?"

"No," he said honestly. "You scared me spitless." He had said something that ordinary! "You scared me so much that I didn't know how to go on with you. I was always so awed just seeing you in the house. You were serene and you knew exactly how to make the computer behave, the house perfect, the meals delicious and me contented. You rattled me. I was afraid I'd rock the boat, and you'd see how ordinary I was."

"Was?" Her questioning tone was deadly. "You're smoother now?"

He studied her question as he looked out through the lacy mesquites without seeing them. His deadlock on her body and legs was just something he had been doing to quieten her, and with the direction their conversation had opened up, he'd forgotten that limitation.

He said, "No. I'm not smooth, not in the interchange between sexes to which you're referring. I really figured once I got you nailed down, I could let you go free...enough...so that you could fly on your own as long as you came to me for your needed attentions."

Almost bitterly, she clarified his thinking, "I needed more than sex."

"How could you minimize what we had? You were...you *are* something magic. You scare me a whole lot. When are you coming home?"

She moved her shoulders to indicate he was to release her. He did not. She replied to his question bluntly, "Being with you was never being 'at home' as my parents were at home. You and I shared a house. I took care of it, fixed your meals, met with the faculty wives and saw that your clothes were fresh—and I went to school."

He straightened it out. "We were married and you shared my bed."

"Now," she told him quite coldly, "I believe that was tuition."

Some disgusted, he mused aloud, "I wonder why my mother never allowed me to smack a female."

"She's a very nice female herself," Jo declared. "She understood that men are bigger. They hit harder?"

Chad remembered, "My dad told me never to strike a woman or a man who was smaller. My mother said, no couth man ever raised his hand to a woman." Chad asked his ex-wife, "Didn't your dad ever discipline you?"

Dangerously stiffened, she suggested, "Are you saying that I was raised—undisciplined? And that was our problem?"

He slowly shook his head once as he frowned but he did say, "You're not docile." That was definitely a criticism. "You're independent and want everything your way." He regarded her in censure.

She tilted her head back and looked at him, so close that she was about cross-eyed. "So now we hear what was the matter in our marriage."

"What?" He frowned down at her.

"You wanted everything your way."

"Well." He pushed up his lower lip and frowned as he considered that. "Yeah." And he smiled at her trapped in his arms and with one leg over her lap holding her down.

She told him, "I believe I could accept your competition over your disregard."

He was indignant. "I could never have disregarded you! My whole day was spent carefully so that I could get everything done and get home to you. There I could talk to you and tell you what all bothered me and who all worried me and what all I'd done."

He even partially released her in order to gesture. "I'm like a bower bird. While I didn't build you a bower nest of flowers, I strutted and showed off to you. Didn't you even notice me? I needed your approval."

She was quite amazed. Had she been so immature that she hadn't realized the support he needed? Was he insecure? How could he be?

She looked into her ex-husband's eyes and told him, "I'm getting cramped. Let me go."

"Oh." He was surprised. "Sorry." He released her. "What can I rub to revive your circulation?"

"Not there."

"Here?" he asked earnestly concerned.

"Not there, either. Cut it out."

Chad protested kindly, "I like doing that."

"You're very skilled," she commented. "Who've you been practicing on?"

He managed a ghost smile of plight as he said in a hollow voice, "Memories."

Was she touched by that? No. She looked down her nose at him and sassed, "People name their children so oddly, nowadays, just who is this—" She stopped herself. Then she said in a stilted manner, "Sorry. It's no longer my concern."

He frowned at her. "Where did you learn such sass? You used to be such a docile child."

She tilted her head several ways. "I've grown up." She grated the words.

He had to agree. "Mentally. But you've still got that great body. You take good care of yourself."

"How interesting that you're surprised I can speak, but you recognize my shape." Then she threw in the ringer. "What were you concentrating on when we were together?"

He lifted his head back and was serious. "I spent all my time trying to impress you."

She gestured openly. "You did. In bed. Most of the time."

"I was trying to mark you as mine and exhaust you so that you wouldn't go looking for another man."

Exasperated, she told him, "I didn't have one. Why would I look for 'another' one?"

He scowled at her and his voice was serious. "Why didn't you mention your loneliness then?"

She could only stare.

Eventually he sorted it out. He agreed, "I talked. I didn't listen." Then he became visually earnest. "I was trying to include you in my life so that you could know me and with what all I had to contend. I shared."

"Sure. Let go of me."

Surprised, he asked, "Oh, aren't you comfortable?" Then he continued to hold her. "I like this bonding. You feel so good against me." And he closed his eyes and hugged her to him.

"Move."

"I can remember you lying under me and saying that very thing." As if that reminded him, he said in great delight, "Let's do that now. Nobody's anywhere around. Let me."

"We need to find an airport."

"Let's find one to hang glide. Would you like to jump off a cliff with me and soar?"

"I get the glider part."

He looked at her quizzically, "Would you let me fall?"

With unromantic irritation, she replied, "Of course not."

"Would you think I would let go of you?"

"No."

"Then you do understand that we are melded and one."

Exasperated, she shook her head as she agreed, "One...mess. We are not together, Chad. If you do remember, we are divorced."

"Our meeting at the Dallas-Fort Worth airport was fate. We belong together."

"It didn't work then—it wouldn't now."

He offered, "We're both more mature."

She watched him still almost eye to eye. "You've forgotten that I'm sterile."

"Then why have we been using condoms?" He was taken aback.

"How many women have you had in the last almost four years, that you've forgotten such a basic fact about me so that you automatically used condoms?''

With a low voice, he told her, ''I wanted to protect you. It was such a gift to be with you again. I didn't want any harm to come to you.''

''None can, unless you're diseased.''

''No.'' He shook his head one serious time. ''I've had no other woman.''

With some surprise, she asked, ''How'd you fight them all off for four years?''

''Just over three years.'' He again corrected her. ''I couldn't see anyone else. I didn't notice anyone who might have been trying to come on to me. If one had tried, she wasn't you, and I couldn't see her.'' Then he asked, ''How many men have you lured to you?''

She lifted her eyebrows and sassed, ''Uhhh, let's see. It's been four years—''

''Just over three.''

Ignoring him, she went right on, ''So it must be close to forty, give or take a few.''

He considered her, and she returned his stare.

He knew she lied.

He said, ''Well, let's see what all you can teach me.'' And in that impossible, cramped space, on the front seat of the car, for Pete's sake, he adroitly turned and shifted and slid and opened clothing, and by golly, he found out.

It was the usual remarkable encounter. Her body loved him, she wiggled to get closer and she made hungry sounds.

His breathing was harsh and his hands were demanding and excessively familiar. His mouth was glued to her hungry mouth. They could still breathe, but it was shiveringly erotic.

They went up the vortex of forever and rockets went off in their heads and in other places. They gasped and strained and mated with exuberance.

They fell back to earth quite gently while still in disassembled chaos. They lay like tossed dolls which had no real use, not anymore. And they lay inert, practicing breath control, giving their hearts time to adjust to normal workings.

As they readjusted their clothing, inept and languid, she asked her ex-husband, "How did you learn to do it that way, on the front seat of a car?"

"You taught me."

She became indignantly hostile. "Hah! You've just trapped yourself. We've never before done it in a car."

Gently, he corrected, "You inquired how I'd managed on the front seat of a car. You taught me because you always pushed me clear over to the bed rail, snuggling and squirming against me. It was from that impossible position that I did my best to give you what you wanted. There is a real similarity between the edge of a bed and a car's front seat."

She considered his explanation and accused him, "You're sly."

He turned his head aside as he raised empty hands in modest protest. "No, no. I'm innovative. I was always willing. I just had to solve how you wanted me. I learned to cope with your demands."

She guessed, "Everything that happened between us was all my fault."

He accepted her confession as he nodded. "Yeah. You looked at me with those big, hungry eyes, but you wouldn't, not until I married you and made it legal. You were so greedy! You exhausted me."

She pulled her skirt under her bottom and finished adjusting her other pushed-aside clothing. She glanced at him a time or two, but she had no response.

In those early days, before they married, she had wanted him. She had thought she was so subtle that he would never know her crush. It had shocked her that everyone on campus had known about them. About her. About how she'd never been able to take her eyes off him. She'd been that obvious.

It had just been a good thing that he'd been susceptible to her.

Throughout the rest of TEXAS, they saw every single stone marking place and read every single historical marker. He took notes.

She was patient and interested. She looked around at the wide-open spaces, lifting her face to the warm TEXAS winter sun and the breezes which denied it was winter.

In all that time, they passed not one single commercial airport. They didn't go through one big city or even near to one. Chad was a crafty man.

So they went over into Oklahoma's western skyways, over the rolling, mostly treeless prairie and on up into a similar Kansas.

She mentioned several times, "How about a train?"

"None close."

"A Greyhound bus?"

"Don't be so impatient." He frowned over at her. "You have to know the country isn't fully settled, yet."

"Those empty lands aren't for settling. They don't have water."

He instructed her, "They spray crops with water. You've seen the circles of green."

"That's irreplaceable water from the Midwest's underground lake that is being siphoned up, and it'll be used up just like that in the part of North Africa, which is now the Sahara Desert. This whole middle America will be a desert. They're on the brink of it in Arizona and New Mexico right now. Too many people, too little water."

He soothed her. "We'll figure a way to use seawater."

"And what will we do with all the salt extracted from the seas?"

He glanced at her briefly so that she could see his disgust before he told her, "When we were first married, and I answered your questions, you weren't this picky."

"This is the real me."

He said, "Hah!" as if something he'd always thought had been confirmed. "You hid it well."

So she felt free to counter, "If you'd been around more then, you wouldn't be so boggled now."

"Nothing boggles me."

Her voice was sad. "I do."

"Actually, you're right. You've tilted me ever since you came in to sign up for my class in World History 101."

"I was there by mistake. I thought it was an English class."

"It took me an hour of talk, lunch and a walk around campus—showing you where what was—to convince you to take my class."

"You were so magical."

He grinned. "Did you think so?"

She looked over at him. "You know that full well. That day, I could have left anytime."

"You kept trying."

"Only pretending. I was testing you."

"Yeah." He was thoughtfully silent before he told her, "But then, I really thought that was what you were doing when you said you were leaving me. I knew you needed some time without me monitoring you, but I hadn't really understood that you were determined to go away by yourself."

She admitted, "I'd already had the job interview."

"I hadn't known that, then." Chad's voice was very low and serious. "I didn't know until Jeff told me he'd seen you being interviewed. I thought you were experimenting with the system. I figured we'd go away for a weekend, and that would solve your restlessness."

"A wife's—restlessness." She tasted the word. "That's an odd labeling of a husband's neglect."

"I thought I had you captured and secure," he told her in an amazed way. "It never occurred to me that you'd break out and run away."

"I told you I was leaving." She lifted her hands. "I told you that after I had my degree. If you remember, you were the one who talked me into staying and getting my master's."

"I really thought you'd start teaching. I know Williams talked to you about that."

She shifted and looked out the car window. "I'm not a teacher. I haven't control."

"You control me."

She was disgusted. "How can you possibly say something that incredible?"

"Well, look at me now! I've called in and canceled, and I've been running around the countryside with you like a restless vagabond."

"This time with you has been as I always wanted it to be." Then she went on sadly, "It's a fluke. I do understand that's so."

He honestly had no reply to that. But he squinted his eyes as he watched the oncoming road, and his mind worked very carefully.

They crossed the Mississippi on a high, charmingly curlicued iron, two-way bridge, before they drove through Tennessee and Kentucky and on north into Indiana. How he had found the byways was beyond Jo. They never saw a four-lane highway. They saw some fast-food places but then, they're everywhere.

Chad asked, "Will you stay with me for a while? Can you take leave from your job for just a while? It would be interesting for you to see how much we've done in the last few years. You haven't asked, but I'm an associate professor now. I have a grad student who is quite good. He's taken over for me in this time that I've found in order to be with you."

At twenty-eight, a woman is on the cutting edge. She said, "I'm surprised you've allowed that. You've allowed someone else to teach your classes. You've always assumed control."

He smiled kindly. "Only with nubile wives." He considered and added, "With students." That was an obvious assumption. "And on occasion with strangers. Otherwise, I'm pliant and courteous."

She laughed ruefully.

He glanced over at her to smile at her before his attention returned to the road. "Your laughter is something else I've missed."

Curiosity made her ask, "What else was there about me that you missed?"

"Coming home to you."

"I had classes." She shrugged. "I wasn't always there."

"Not lately at all. I've missed you."

"Baloney."

Four

It was while Chad and Jo were driving through the snowy back roads of picture book, southern Indiana that he asked her once again, "Will you come stay with me for a while?"

She was looking around and replied casually off-hand. "I might."

And he was so thrilled by her tentative reply that he was afraid to say or ask anything else.

The city of Indianapolis, Indiana, harbors just over one million people. It's the size of San Antonio, TEXAS. Oddly, Indianapolis appears to be less hectic than San Antonio. It is probably because San Antonio is greatly older and the growth is more hodgepodge. There is a saying in TEXAS that five hundred years ago, San Antonio was laid out by a drunk man on a blind mule.

Jo hadn't been in Indianapolis in almost four years. She looked around as they drove through the snowy streets. "I'd forgotten that," she'd say. She'd say, "I remember that." And she'd say, "This part is almost like Chicago."

Chad smiled and glanced at her.

Then they went up Meridian's four-lane street, and she was surprised that it looked the same. The Children's Museum was there. The preserved great old houses were mostly used by businesses or societies, but several were still occupied by families. The vacant apartment buildings were being renovated as offices.

Finally, finally, America was finding it could renovate instead of abandoning. It seemed possible that people could learn to care for things instead of allowing them to slowly slip into abandonment.

For want of a nail— From that fragment, Jo's mind went on to consider that although the rhyme was about a lost horseshoe, and an undelivered message in war, it applied to anything that needed care. That included saving a government, or a building or a child before it was lost to carelessness.

Before Chad took her to his house, he drove her through the campus at Butler University. As usual, the tidy, beautiful campus of learning was heart lifting to Jo. It had given her the opportunity to learn, and she had.

Butler was named for an attorney who was an abolitionist. It was open to students in 1855. From the beginning, all peoples were welcome there to learn. It was the second university in the nation to employ a woman as a full professor.

Chad drove on through the snowy campus. The streets and walks had been cleared and shoveled. There were some ordinary snowmen but there were inventive sculptures. There had probably been a competition.

Butler was in the northern part of the city, which had enveloped the campus and gone on beyond. The buildings are attractive and the campus is picturesque.

Chad's rented car slowly left the campus. Chad glanced over at Jo, who was silent and watching where they were. He drove along the canal on the west side of the campus, which continues across to the east, where the ducks are given first choice and cars stop when the ducks choose to cross the street. At one place, there is a legal Duck Crossing sign.

Gina Stephens has been one who helped feed the ducks in winter. Now the stores in the Broad Ripple section along the canal have counter bottles for donations to feed the ducks.

Along the canal, the ducks rule. They investigate the yards of the houses along the canal. In the spring they make nests in those yards or along the banks of the canal.

The ducks allow the humans to proliferate and build beyond their territory, but the ducks are complacent the canal belongs to them.

Chad's house was east of the campus on the street named Kenwood. The house was brick and appeared smaller than it was. Even though she had rejected being a part of it, Jo remembered the house quite clearly. How strange to come back to a place that she had given up. It was Chad's house. She'd given him up at the same time.

How had circumstances evolved so that she had come back, along with him and to the house?

Chad brought his car to a stop in the snowy driveway and looked over at Jo. "Welcome home."

She gave him a patient, rueful look.

His smile was vulnerable as he said, "Sit still. Let me open the door for you."

Her ear registered the fact that his voice was the rather roughened tone of emotion. What was she doing there at that place and with him?

She bit her lip as her mind replied all sorts of things. None of the self-scoldings was kind. She had no business there. She had left for good reason. She should have stayed away.

But— How could she have left the car on those deserted highways to thumb a ride? He had never found a motel until after dark. What choices had she had then? Stay with him or hitchhike in this chancy time?

So there she was with a rejected husband and a house she'd abandoned. How strange it was to be there.

His steps crunched in the evening snow as he came around the car and opened the car door.

How can a man's face be so male and so vulnerable at the same time?

Damn.

She ignored the offered hand and slid out of the car. The neighbor's yellow, thick-haired, winter-loving, lame tomcat limped over the snow into their— Chad's—yard and looked at the arrivals aloofly before he licked in boredom.

She said so offhandedly, "See you still got the same old cat."

That was the legend greeting from a small boy who ran away from home but wasn't allowed to cross the street so he'd gone around the block a couple of times. When he came inside, no one appeared to notice him and the boy's opening comment was the one Jo mistakenly used.

Chad gasped as he grinned, and his emotional, "You're home!" twisted in Jo's vitals. She'd needlessly implied she was back. It was cruel to mislead Chad.

As they entered the house, she noted as he reversed the card on the door from *enter* to *scram!*

In the living room, she looked around and observed coolly, "It's still the same old mess."

He grinned widely and replied the usual, "It's a challenge."

She shook her head. "The whole mess looks just the same."

He alibied. He had always had an alibi. The papers were being separated for filing. Or he was sorting out the more important items for a book. Or he was doing research. This time, he said, "I've been away."

She slid a glance at him and inquired, "While you were gone, it all proliferated?"

"By golly, you could be right!"

Her comment had been a quote of his. She'd heard it all before.

She looked around the untidy house and then back at the magical man. She began to remember more about the debit side.

She said, "If you've brought me here to organize and file all this, forget it. I've done my stint of that."

"No. I brought you here to lure you back to me."

She stared at him, incredulous. She gave an impressive, all-inclusive movement of her hand as she replied, "I've been here." Then she raised her eyebrows a tad as she softened her voice to remind him, "I left."

His face was sober. As they stood there, still in their coats, their luggage still in the car, his reply was serious. He said, "When I saw you in the airport, I couldn't believe it was you. My heart almost went on overload. I couldn't breathe. I worked my way over to you to see if you were real and not an imagined hologram.

"It was you, and you were just as magical as you've always been. I tried to think of any way that I could get your attention and keep it. If the pilot hadn't spoken then, I have no idea what sort of jackass I'd have appeared to be.

"To get you alone, and to remind you of our love was the greatest gift I've ever had. I love you with all my heart and soul."

"Yeah."

"Now, Jo, how can you be so cynical when I've bared my soul to you?"

"There are people with different needs. I don't believe we've ever actually meshed."

"Give it a try. I'll be around more. I'll see to it. You'll be reintroduced to the better part of our lives." He looked around fondly at the litter and promised her, "I'll pay some of the smarter students to file these. I know a couple who have the time and ability to do it. They need the cash. I promise."

Jo mentioned thoughtfully, "I've never seen the furniture under all this."

"Now, Jo, you know you have. Remember when it was our turn to entertain the faculty?"

She nodded as her pupils widened. "What a nightmare!"

"It was fun!"

"Yeah. Sure."

"It was." He was sure. "Everyone had a great time."

"As I recall, just before the date of our party, you were selected to go to DePauw to teach a seminar."

"Yeah. That was really something for me at that time. I was so raw and—"

"I did the cleaning and assembling and shopping and cooking and—"

He put in, "I chose the—"

"The flowers and—"

He smiled kindly and said with some positive agreement, "It was a stretching experience for you."

Sourly, remembering, Jo said falsely, "I was so grateful for it." Then she thought of the first office party she'd had thrown in her lap to organize and oversee. And she was honest to Chad. "Actually, it really was a help. After that, nothing sundered me."

"See?" He grinned.

She guessed. "Our marriage was training in survival . . . alone."

He frowned thoughtfully. "While we lived together, you felt . . . alone?"

"I was."

With a serious face, he took her coat from her shoulders and then tried to find a hanger in the stuffed coat closet.

She suggested, "It'll be okay on the sofa back. I'll be leaving shortly."

His head jerked up and his face was stark. She knew what he'd looked like as a child in the dark. She frowned. Why would he care?

And she figured he'd forgotten about their lives together. He just recalled the sex.

While she had had no additional, widening experience, sex with Chad had always been superb. However, although she realized that, she remembered too much of the ninety-eight percent of the debit side of their marriage.

The littered downstairs was one.

If she hadn't organized and filed his papers, the whole house would have looked then as it did now... or worse.

Actually, it was probably her fault. If she hadn't organized his papers, he might well have had to find a way to do it.

She said, "It would be better if I leave. I can't stay here in this mess. And I—"

"Let me make a couple of calls. Then I'll take your bags upstairs."

He was no longer feeling vulnerable; he was again in control.

He thought he was. He'd forgotten all the training she'd had because of him. If she hadn't been married to Chad, she wouldn't have that knowledge, the schooling or her present job. She'd had a free ride in her degrees. She'd had good sex and a good education. And she'd learned to cook.

So. Maybe she owed him some time? She'd . . . see.

Jo sat carefully on the pillow of the sofa, which Chad had cleared with some bemused concentration on exactly where to put the moved papers. He needed a class in office organization. They offered a very good one in Butler's School of Business. She'd taken it.

He then made three phone calls. And as he talked to each one, he explained what he needed, what he would pay and inquired about availability.

Since it was early in the term, there were organized upper grade students who needed the money. And he hired all three.

He hung up the phone and said to Jo, "I'll have to get some cabinets for the back room."

He made another call. It was to a professor whose offices were to be renovated and there were some cabinets to be discarded. The two dickered in a very nice manner, and each felt he'd made a good deal. He dickered for two.

Listening, Jo shook her head and held up all five fingers.

Chad frowned at Jo, then he slid in the fact to the professor that, as a favor, he'd take five of the file cabinets.

When he hung up, he looked at Jo, very pleased he was trying to please her. In controlling the paper, specifically for Jo, Chad felt he'd sundered a giant just for her.

But she said, "I'll pay for the cabinets as my host gift."

That wobbled him a bit. She could pay out that much so casually? With a frown, he asked, "How much do you make?"

She shrugged fractionally then turned out one hand in a dismissive manner as she replied, "Enough."

Chad stood watching her with his head tilted back a bit. He was evaluating her as he would the potential of a student.

She returned his regard with the same kind of tolerance.

That was probably what most boggled Chad. She was no longer a student. She was a full adult. An equal. In some things, she knew more than he.

The good part was that he didn't feel diminished. He, too, was adult. He was stimulated by her confidence and mature ease. In his field of teaching, he dealt with too many young people who hadn't yet acquired the ease of being truly adult. Their time would come.

Chad had had to be the leader, the confidant . . . the teacher. It would be interesting to know this bed partner as an equal.

He said to his guest, "I'll go get your luggage."

"I haven't that much." She rose from the only empty seating place in the room.

"You forget Mexico."

She laughed. "Ah, yes. I was rash. When will I ever get to wear those things?"

"You can here."

She shook her head. "Not until summer. Mexico doesn't understand about winter."

He lifted his eyebrows quite humorously. "The leather and sheep's-wool lined vests?"

"You have a point." Then she said, "I can go to a motel. I'll keep the rental car while I'm here."

That she could keep a rental car so casually tightened his scalp. "I insist. Stay here. There's your room for you here."

"I don't like intruding."

He shook his head to deny intrusion. "This is your place, too. You're here."

She considered. Then she said slowly, "Only for a day or so."

"We'll see."

And she recalled he had been such a marvelous companion in those past days. It had been as she'd hoped, long ago. What if he had changed and now could share their lives? Was it possible?

So she said, "A day or so."

They went out to the car and brought their things back into the house.

He put his luggage and bags down and again one thudded. She recalled that happening at the hotel. What on earth did he carry that was so heavy?

He reached for her burdens as he said, "Let me have them."

"Where am I to sleep?" She gave him a considering study.

"Your room."

She'd always had a room of her own. It was at the top of the stairs. He slept with her because he couldn't find anyplace in his room. His room looked like the entire downstairs, cluttered, piled with books and papers. It was disheartening to any observer.

But for him, it was a room-size filing cabinet. He knew where everything was. How amazing such chaos could have any order at all. And she noted all the strange weights which kept the disciplined papers from flying with an opened door or window.

She knew that if she had stayed, by now "her room" would be just like the rest of the house.

So why did she climb the stairs, carrying some of her purchases? Why didn't she just go on and go to a motel? There was a string of them not far away, just west of St. Vincent's hospital.

After she viewed the disaster of what had been her room, she would be firm in that she'd go to a motel. She was not committed to this man just because he used to be her husband and she had freely traveled with him down to Mexico.

She found what had been her room was pristine.

How shocking.

She stood and looked around in silent amazement.

He lay her bag on the bed and added her purchases. She put her purse on the old bureau, which had a mounted tilting mirror. The top had been dusted.

"It's been dusted?"

"Mrs. Stoic does that. I hired her after you—left me."

"She...cleans?" How could any human voice hold such doubt?

Gesturing to indicate to what area he referred, Chad said, "She limits her cleaning to this room. The kitchen. And she does the washing and ironing."

Jo looked around. "Too bad you don't add another room or two to the cleaning list."

Chad shrugged. "I did. She declined."

Jo had to laugh.

He complained, "Until you left, I hadn't realized all you did around here. When did you have the time?"

She shrugged. "It was either get it cleaned up or give up entirely."

He smiled at her. "I sleep in here."

"I won't inquire why that would be."

"Even if you aren't here, I sleep in here."

"Close the door to your room. I don't believe I can handle seeing it."

"I did when I first came up."

"Where can I put my things?"

"None of my stuff is in this room. I've been waiting for you to come home."

She opened the closet door. It held only hangers. Jo looked at him.

His regard was serious.

She opened the drawers in the bureau and the chest, and it was as he said. They were all empty.

She regarded him soberly.

He came to her and said softly, "Welcome home."

Her return gaze was neutral as she told him, "I'm only visiting."

He smiled. "We'll see."

After tucking her few clothes and accoutrements into the empty drawers, Jo stood at the bedroom window and looked out over the backyards. The bare limbed trees were decorated with snow. The winds hadn't been strong enough to clean the garage roofs or loosen the snow caught in the tree branches.

Jo remembered the backyard view. It wasn't one she'd particularly cherished or recalled, but now it was touchingly familiar.

The scene was unfairly lovely. It gave her a twinge of homesickness for a place she'd discarded almost four years before.

She heard the doorbell. And listened as voices came into the house. It was undoubtedly the three-man crew Chad had gathered. They were already there? She lifted her chin and commanded her sentimentally weakened backbone to straighten up.

She considered the neat bed and was tempted to take a nap. She was not going downstairs and help with the cleanup. Probably the best thing she could do was go over to the shopping area. It was a familiar place.

She put on her coat and picked up her shoulder bag. She went down the stairs to the hall and into the kitchen. She checked the refrigerator and the shelves. They could use about anything.

So she went into the living room where the crew was busily sorting papers. Chad was not there.

There were three students. Jo introduced herself and learned their names.

Sam was one of the young men. Trevor gave her an adult look, saw that she was dressed to go out and said, "Chad went to get the file cabinets. He took my truck. The car keys are on the table in the hall."

She nodded pleasantly as she said, "Good luck on this mess."

The one who had a female voice was Natalie. She commented, "Chad is so learned."

Such an earnest compliment. Jo observed the dedicated student and replied, "Yeah."

So the young, budding women were still mesmerized by Chad. Jo knew the feeling well.

She told those in the room, "I'll be back. Anything you'd like for supper?"

"He's already told us to get our own and leave you two to yourselves." Sam grinned. So did Trevor. However, the silent Natalie studied Jo with competitive eyes.

Jo gave her a "good gravy" look and went out the door.

Having been a Chicago woman for several years after living in Indianapolis for six years, Jo had boots.

She'd packed them to wear from O'Hare when she got back from her holiday.

Jo drove the rental car to Keystone at the Crossing and purchased some northern clothing, a flannel nightgown, a suit, some slacks and a hat.

She drove back to the compound of shops on Illinois at 56th Street. At a grocery, she selected the food for that evening. She also bought her favorite cereal and some milk to take home.

Home?

It was Chad's place.

She would do better if she would call the fact to her attention every now and then.

Just because he was a wondrous lover was no reason—at all—for her to become entangled again. What she ought to do was to get out of there and go back to Chicago.

Yeah.

However, he was on a roll of cleaning up and filing all that mess. She really ought to stick around until that was under control. Mmm-hmm. She should.

So she went to the florist shop and bought some holly branches left over from Christmas and handled it all very carefully. And she drove back to—Chad's house.

She looked around, breathing the air, feeling...she was in a familiar place. It was like going back home and seeing it again but not being committed to staying.

She felt sure she would not be there for very long. How interesting. She'd been uneasy that Chad's fantastic lovemaking would be lure enough. But what would she do while he was revitalizing?

Jo remembered how she'd spent her time in Indy. The classes wouldn't be repeated. That was past. But Chad appeared to still be on the treadmill of teaching and there was his dedication to his students.

It would be interesting to see how long he'd stick around to share time with her. She considered. She'd give him five days. Before the five days were past, she figured, he'd have sorted priorities and be back in his routine. He'd vanish for most of the time.

If they'd still been married, his distraction would have been that day. Of course, he wasn't at his house right then. He was away collecting the cabinets. She would bet he'd make an earnest effort to be around her for a while.

Five days was the long count.

As she approached the intersection for Kenwood, she saw the newly hired crew was helping take the cabinets into the house.

Jo parked the car on the street. Sam and Trevor were busy outside with Chad. Natalie was stacking and carrying the papers into the file room-to-be.

Chad helped Jo carry the groceries into the kitchen and she found a large empty peanut butter jar to hold the holly. She placed it in the middle of the cluttered dining room table. How droll.

How telling. She with her touches of color or art, and he with the onslaught of paper.

Actually, the holly was a lovely accent and made the papers look as if they were there only temporarily.

Chad followed Jo back into the kitchen and said, "The holly is such a nice touch. I didn't realize until now why the house was always so dreary after you left."

"See? You should have just gotten some flowers!"

"It's you." His throat clacked like a young man's. "Don't."

He blinked and frowned a little. Then he looked at her packages and asked, "What did you get?"

"Supper. You don't have anything in the refrigerator."

"I got us a couple of steaks." He opened the refrigerator door. He'd added a carton of milk, vegetables— "I remembered you like those."

When had he ever thought of going to a grocery store? Once when she'd had the flu. How surprising it was that he'd chosen now to shop. But then, he'd had to think of food now and again after she'd left.

She saw that he'd also brought home fruit and a frozen cake with icing.

Her diet had changed considerably in almost four years. She nodded and said, "You can have one of the steaks tonight."

He was serious. "One is for you."

"I rarely eat meat."

He was shocked. "I've heard of people like you."

She denied being selective with the alternating reply, "Of course there is McDonald's."

"Ahhhh. Of course." He grinned at her. "We had a lot of those three years ago."

"It was before that. By the time I'd left you, almost four years ago, my own tastes had changed."

Rather bitterly he responded, "Yes."

Before she could tell Chad she was talking about diet, one of the male tidiers called, "Chad?"

Chad told Jo, "I'll be back."

There was an instant, familiar ring to the words. She remembered an anniversary when she'd fallen asleep on the living room sofa as she'd waited for his return.

He'd come back and called to her from upstairs as he opened and closed doors. He'd come downstairs as she was rising from the sofa. He'd kissed her and laid her back on it as he'd taken her. She'd responded about like a rag doll.

Ah, youth and sex. Mmm-hmm.

She put some scrubbed potatoes into the oven to bake. With the carton of milk, she'd bought onion-flavored yogurt.

She prepared the meal's salad, then sliced one piece from the cake and put it aside in the fridge to thaw enough. She marinated the steak in a mix of oil and onion with peppercorns.

It felt strange to again be in that kitchen and planning a meal for Chad. She looked out the window at the snow and her face was serious.

Five

In the kitchen, Jo delayed the dinner. That was familiar. She put Chad's steak back into the refrigerator. Then she finally snacked from the salad, toasted a roll and spread it with peanut butter. And all the while, the entire process was a reminder of having done the same thing times on end.

Chad was a good argument for a woman to experience living with a man before she committed to marriage. No sex. Just experiencing a man's normal conduct when he wasn't in the courting mode.

She remembered all the attention he'd given her during the time he tried to mesmerize her enough to get her into bed. He had been gaunt and honed and mostly slept through their honeymoon.

The long, honeymoon weekend had been quite boring. As Chad slept, Jo learned to tat with a shuttle, taught by an elderly woman who was enjoying the air.

Whoever believes she will learn a skill on her honeymoon? Well, another kind of skill.

And, having nailed her in with a wedding ring, Chad had returned to his chosen way of living. It hadn't really included her. Why did Jo so foolishly think it could be different—now?

She had her own field of endeavor. By now, Chad had a very current computer. Jo went to his upstairs chaotic office and squinched her eyes so that she saw only the computer. Such talent was called "seeing selectively." She had learned that skill living with Chad.

Through the computer, Jo contacted her office. She said, *I'll be here for five or six days and I am available.* She also gave Chad's phone number.

Her company had computer programs that were very good. Some were a little intense. There are just some people who do not read with instant comprehension. They need to be led along. That can be done over the phone; she led them with her own visual of their problem on her own computer. She could do the same using Chad's.

Having given her office her location, she said goodbye, shut off the machine and went downstairs to find that Chad had gone to his office for a box of file folders.

The crew had eaten everything in sight. Jo tidied the kitchen.

Déjà vu.

Upstairs, she stood in the tub for a long shower. Then she found her new flannel nightgown, took it from its plastic sheath and found all the pins that held it so rigidly. She put on the gown, brushed her teeth and went to bed. To sleep perchance to dream.

Her body was weary and sexually sated. She needed an off night. She sank into sleep that was deep and dreamless.

Well, for a while.

As in a dream, Jo first heard the breathing. Then the bed moved and there was the distant, rustling sounds of the bed covers. The breathing was closer, next to her and then the heat of his body engulfed her.

She was so deep in sleep that the entire happening was—distanced. A dream. His hard, skin-rough hands scrubbed her body, relishing it. His breathing was broken as if he was winded from the long ordeal of reaching her . . . finally.

How could he be so intense after such a concentrated sexual week? Actually, it'd been almost ten days.

Why wasn't he grateful just to be in bed and go to sleep?

He moved her so that she was curled against his body, her bottom against his excited lap. His breaths gusted hotly and his hands squeezed and rubbed.

Her sleep-drugged mind was shocked that her disinterested bottom squirmed lasciviously against his ardent arousal. She was naked? Where was her new flannel nightgown? Her sublevel consciousness thought it must not be a real happening, it must be some erotic dream.

Sated women do not dream erotica. They sleep deeply and don't dream at all.

Her mouth moaned with need.

She heard it! It did!

How shocking!

The hoarsely breathing male was curled, pressing around on her body. He laughed softly, deep in his throat, in a perfectly wicked manner. His hands moved in hard swirls, kneading, rubbing, feeling, caressing as they explored the contours of her susceptible body. And her breathing was so that her lips had to part for her to gasp.

But then reality occurred to Jo. How could he "explore" something so well-known?

He leaned up in the bed, allowing the cold air to come under the blanket. Instead of making her shiver, it was refreshing. Her already parted lips smiled a little. Her eyelids were too heavy to lift so that she could see him. But her body knew he was there with her.

He looked down her nakedness, which he could see in the reflection of the snow from outside. Then his breaths scalded her as he leaned his mouth to her nipples. He nipped them with tightened lips and slathered them with his wet tongue before he suckled, pulling the sensitive elongated buds deep into his hot mouth. His scalding tongue stroked the underside of the nipple as it was pressed against the roof of his mouth.

The whole encounter shivered Jo's sensual nerve ends and excited her entire body... even her spread toes. She made little sounds. Her hands were in his hair, holding his mouth there to pleasure her. But he didn't mind having her hold his head. He wasn't in any hurry.

His hand found its way to the crisp curls which demurely covered her alluring secrets. His hand moved over the crinkling curls and rubbed her as his mouth moved to hers.

His mouth was hot, his kisses were different, deeper, more demanding. It had been a long time since she'd been held and kissed that way. His mouth and tongue played with hers to coax her further into passion.

Chad was wasting his talents. She was already there. She moaned and rubbed against his hand. Her body writhed to call attention to itself.

She had his attention. It was concentrated, intense and narrowed to a point. The point was throbbing and waggling and hard. It was excited and needy.

She moved her chest languidly against his. She wiggled and turned as she groaned. And he laughed huskily with great pleasure.

He was sweating.

There Indianapolis was, in the middle of the worst winter they'd had in almost twenty years, and he was sweating. That was pushy. And he was . . . pushy.

He sought her lure, and it was wet. His laugh was different. Smoky. His throat clacked as he licked his lips. His kiss was then different. Gentle. Coaxing. Luring her.

She was past being lured. She was making little hungry sounds and trying to get closer to him. She was rubbing herself against his hot body so that the hair on his chest was excited. He was excited in other places also.

His toes were curled in stiffened concentration of his straightened member. He slid his big hands under her bottom to cup and grasp as he kneaded those rounds.

He put one hand between her knees and ran the tips of his fingers up the sensitive skin on the insides of her thighs.

The recently sated woman under his chest writhed and began to pull at his shoulders.

His hair trembled with his intense control. Breathing through parted lips, his breaths were broken and his concentration was riveted.

She was just about frantic.

He parted her knees so that he could slide into her hot sheath. He paused as she gasped and shivered. She wanted him so badly.

It would have been easy to have just gone on, but he hesitated and kept her from moving. Encased, burning, he shivered.

And it was only then that she understood his control. His giving of pleasure. She looked at him, and he lifted his head to return her regard. He was so serious.

So was she.

Jo touched his cheek with gentle fingers and her gaze was one of "seeing" him. She was caught in the fact that he was human. That he was a male human being. And he had needs and compassion beyond what she'd understood.

How strange it was for her to regard him as a separate person. And she was compassionate. She lifted her mouth, and their kiss was different from any contact they'd ever experienced.

And the lovemaking became different. It didn't lessen. It stayed intense. But their delicious caresses and sensual movements were sweetly gentle with the bonding of exquisite sharing.

Their exchanges were gentled, their kisses sweeter. Their writhings were the curlings of a kind of bed dance. They pleasured each other, touching, smoothing, caressing, feeling.

Their strokings were erotic. They separated to lie in their dream of love. They held hands and smiled. The passion was hot, but it wasn't the primal act it had always been. It was different. More caring.

They moved and touched and kissed. They coupled slowly and gently rubbed as they moved. Their bed dance progressed, and it was exquisite. It was also incredible they hadn't climaxed.

When they did reach that peak, it was slow and spectacular. It was a time of incredible fulfillment for their bodies.

It was remarkable. Besides the basic act of sex, they had truly made love.

As they lay completely lax in the languid exhaustion of marvelous completion, Chad said, "Ahhh... my wife."

She replied lazily, "Actually, I'm only a temp mistress."

"We'll see."

"What will 'we see'?"

He suggested slowly, "Kiss me and let's see if you can stir my embers."

She laughed helplessly. Her small hand spread over his face and she gently pushed at him.

He said the old tattered female comment, "You lose interest so fast."

She sought his lax sex and just waggled it as his body buckled and he said an *oof!* of surprise. "Be careful. Some hungry witch overused it."

She guessed, "It needs to be kissed well?"

"Not right now."

She laughed in soft chuckles.

In a naked, honest voice, he told her, "I've really missed you."

"You've been pure for almost four years?"

"Yes."

She chuckled.

"It's true." His voice was an honest, sober rumble. "I've looked at women at various times, but none of them was you."

"A hot man like you?"

"Have you had—other men?"

"I haven't had the time," she replied with open honesty. "I just talk computer addicts through programs."

"None of them makes any moves on you?"

She was droll as she replied, "It rather irritates them that they're talking to a woman who knows more about the program than they."

He gently gathered her to him. She did resist somewhat, but he just settled her closer to him and in his arms. He said, "I can understand a man having that problem. A man in my shoes knows women are just as smart or smarter. I've seen it firsthand."

"Could you take instruction from me?" she asked with new curiosity.

He replied lazily, "You taught me sex."

"And before me, you'd never tried it?"

He frowned as he thought back over his whole life and with all honesty he told her, "Not that I recall."

So she asked, "Have you forgotten those encounters during the last, almost four years?"

He corrected her, "Just over three years. I did encounter one or two willing female students. They always scare the hell out of the professors. A nubile wreck can tangle up any good man. But none of them reminded me of you. Not even nearly. And I really wasn't even tempted. Not at all. Since I wasn't tempted, you have to realize my love for you is forever."

She scoffed. "You'd come around. It wouldn't take much. The only reason you reject the students is that they are now too young, and you would have to be patient and kind to survive through the training process as you did with me."

He was shocked, "I taught *you?* Now, how can that be when I was also a virgin?"

She scoffed.

"I *was!* I don't remember any other woman ever putting her hand in my pants the way you did."

"I *never!*"

"Yeah? How about the picnic?"

She sputtered and laughed. "We were already *married!*"

"That proves you remember well that I was an innocent. I had to be married before any woman actually unzipped my pants and put her hand inside...seeking   my—poor—frightened—appendage!"

She scoffed. "Do you recall what you'd been doing just before that?"

He replied as if he was on a witness stand and under oath. "I was eating a peanut butter sandwich." In an aside, he explained, "You hadn't yet learned there was more to eating than peanut butter."

"You were not eating, we hadn't even opened the picnic basket! You put your hand up my shirt and grabbed me."

Prissily he reminded her, "I wasn't in your pants, for Pete's sake. I'm not like some! I haven't even given your real name!"

She was giggling and protesting and gasping and probably beet red.

He hugged her. And his voice was breathy as he told her seriously, "I loved it when you were so bold. I'd been half scared of you up until then. I'd done all the luring and loving, and you were so quiet and big-eyed. I wasn't sure you'd like it."

"I thought I might shock you. I didn't know to help you, or that you wanted to be touched."

"I love it. I love you."

She was somewhat pensive as she advised him, "You need to see that there are other women who will be contented to tidy your files, cook you innovative meals and sleep in your bed."

He was silent for a time. She thought he was going to sleep.

He asked, "Are you saying you'd approve of my marrying another woman?"

She sassed, "I'd doubt you'd be comfortable with a man. So a woman would be all that is left. Don't you want children?"

"With you."

Bitterly, she said it again, "I'm sterile, you know that."

"We'll find us a couple of kids who might need parents."

"It's not like the old days. Very few are up for adoption."

"There are kids available. If you were bendable, I'd like them around. It would be nice."

"What you actually mean is that you want some kids to see on occasion, to greet you when you come home. But you expect the wife to care for them, chauffeur them, nurse them when they're sick and train them to be obedient and mind the rules."

"I'd be responsible for my share of the raising."

"Like you file your notes?"

He chided gently, "That was underhanded and unkind."

"But it's true."

He considered a minute. "I could change."

"No. You wouldn't remember to do any of it. You'd be just as you are now, which is exactly as you were when I first married you."

He shifted in the bed and took her more comfortably into his arms. "In the just over three years since you left me, I've changed. I've matured and become more responsible."

"Chad. Chad. It is almost four years. And you know that your changing is not true. You're a superior prof. You care about your students. You're a remarkable lover. However, to be honest, you do have a flaw. You are not tidy. This place is a mess."

"No longer! I have a system."

"Your system does not exist. Your mother blamed me for your lack of orderliness. It wasn't until we had this house and the basement that I realized you were just naturally a mess. I'd hoped you had changed and could cope."

He advised her, "I'm capable of anything. And I can be neat."

"Good luck with it."

He snuggled her closer and sighed. He made relishing sounds of holding her. He said, "I love having you in my bed."

She had to admit it, so she was honest, "You're a fantastic lover."

He said smugly, "I have other talents."

She was not won. "Being tidy isn't one. Even Mrs. Stoic can't really put up with you."

"Do you suppose her stern, blank face is because she married a stoic?"

Jo groaned. Then she retorted, "She is probably just that way because she's seen this house, and it offends her."

"Does it offend you?"

"I left."

He was silent for a while. Then he asked carefully, "Was it my untidiness that drove you away?"

She murmured thoughtfully, "I might have coped with that, but if you will recall, I left here, almost four years ago, because I rarely saw you. These last ten days have been what I thought our marriage would be. It was not. I left."

"But you haven't found a man to replace me...have you?"

"No." She yawned and stretched within his arms. "I've been too busy getting organized."

"Do you get vacations?"

"Of course."

"Where do you go?"

"Around." She gestured to show that. Then she went on to explain, "We mostly go down to Rio or to one of the islands in the Carib. We avoid the unstable places."

"What do you do?"

She shrugged. "We play." Then she elaborated, "We really work hard and a lot of times we go days without any break. When we go to the islands, we play."

"With . . . ?" He waited with some tension.

She replied, "Golf, tennis, swimming—"

"Men?"

She shook her head. "We have enough of them in Chicago."

"You can't tell me that you and some of your cohorts don't line up with male company at resorts."

So, of course, she had to say, "On my honeymoon, I learned to tat."

"That was probably all that saved me from an exquisite death of overusage. You're a greedy woman and a shock to an innocent male."

"Pah!"

He yawned and stretched but took her back against him. "You have no idea how shocking it was to marry an innocent, careful woman and go on a honeymoon. You were so curious! And you cooperated so fast!"

She shrugged. "I'd waited long enough."

"Part of me was exhausted."

"Poor Chad."

"Nobody warned me about women," he complained. "They just rolled their eyes and laughed and punched my shoulder. Nobody mentioned how ravished a man is by a new woman."

"I'd read a very explicit handbook."

"Wow! How come you didn't bring it along on our honeymoon? They must have had some sort of countering in the text?"

"No."

He was aghast. "It was just go ahead and do it—every time?"

She nodded. "Yep."

He was silent, smiling, holding back a laugh. He gave a sigh that was not sincere. "It's just a wonder I survived as well as I did."

She scoffed, "You were mostly a dead bore."

He gasped. "After all I handled?" And his voice squeaked up in shock.

Still disgruntled, she reminded him, "You mostly slept."

He nodded in agreement. Then he had the gall to comment, "Well, you did learn to tat, so the time wasn't entirely wasted."

"The woman who taught me had had a husband very like you. She told me it probably wouldn't get any better. I didn't believe her...then."

He was indignant. "But I did. My track practice helped my survival quite a good deal."

Thoughtfully, she recalled, "I remember the smell of the muscle relaxant."

"It wasn't for that muscle. It was my leg muscles and my back."

"Uh-huh." Her tone was droll.

How could her agreement sound so countering? Elaborately offended, he enunciated, "It *was!*"

"I said, 'Yeah.'"

"It was hoo-doo cream you rubbed into my innocent sex."

She shook her head and said it yet again, "It was an aphrodisiac."

He retorted, "I never understood why you'd need that. If you hadn't been so oversexed that five times a day weren't enough, you should have figured a relief that didn't include me."

"Five—?"

He gasped. "So. It really *was* a dozen? My mind got hazy and I'd lose count?"

She ignored his interruption. "I remember being on my knees, begging, after three weeks."

He laughed. He laughed and laughed. He hugged her and went on laughing, and he proved that his reluctance wasn't true at all, at all. Then he wakened her in the night and proved it again.

So he slept late the next day. She stood by the bed and observed him in his sleep. He looked like a sundered knight who had won the joust. However, he had no early classes.

Jo went downstairs wearing jeans, a flannel shirt and Reeboks. She found Sam and Natalie were there already. They had a key for convenience. One mentioned that Trevor was in class.

Jo made no offer to help file. She greeted the two in passing and received a rather disapproving glance from Natalie, who remained silent.

There were three computer calls that day, for Jo, asking for aid on rebellious computers. As with anything, it's the approach that must be accurate and kind. She carefully led each one through the problem.

She would ask, "What's on your screen now?"

And slowly they would understand. Then she would go back and lead each one through the process twice more.

One man was anticomputer and resistant, but Jo was an excellent convincer of the magic there at his fingertips.

He was another who asked for a personal meeting.

She told him she was in Timbuktu.

He asked, "What state's that in?"

And she replied, "Wyoming." But when she reported back to her supervisor, she asked not to be connected with that customer again.

The supervisor replied, "Why not? So he gets to see Wyoming."

And with undue patience, Jo replied sweetly, "Please."

The supervisor's voice was disgruntled as he responded, "Aw, you always dust off those nasty words on me. No heart."

And she replied heartlessly, "None."

He sighed and said, "Here're your next ones. None is frantic."

She did the first two. One was very simple and just needed a little courage. The other was a miscue. No big deal. So she did the third one and it was a lulu. They had to go back to square one *nine* times!

Jo reeled away from that one to find Chad coming up the stairs. She looked at him cross-eyed and said, "It's all yours."

Then she looked beyond him to Elsie!

She exclaimed, "Else?" And there she was, laughing. Easy. Glad to see Jo.

One thing about Elsie, each time they met, and it had been years by then, it was as if they had never parted. It was like falling into step and going along easily. She was a dear friend.

"So what have you been up to?" Jo asked her friend. "Did you get the silver car?"

"It's green."

"Tad has always had a closed mind. I warned you when we were juniors. But you never would listen to me."

"Oh, I don't know. I did *listen* to you, I just didn't pay any attention to your advice. And Tad is perfect. I say that quite easily, since he's standing down there in the hall and listening."

So Jo went down the stairs, followed by Chad, and the four picked up just as if they had all been together the day before.

Other people came by to see Jo. It was fortunate that one of Chad's great virtues was that he remembered to tell Jo which guest was calling or coming over. On top of that essential characteristic, he reminded her how she'd known the caller.

Jo acknowledged to Chad that in some things he was a superior man.

He said, "Shucks, ma'am," and made his marvelous body shy and humble.

There is just nothing to compare to a sharing, deliberate ham bone... for that particular time. Unfortunately, the times to share had been so limited.

It wasn't until the fourth day that Chad was gone at breakfast. It was odd to waken to a still house. Not even any of the three file experts was around.

Jo hadn't wakened alone since before she'd been in the Dallas-Fort Worth airport all those aeons ago. Well, it was over two weeks. She'd been surrounded by crowds or Chad in all that time, and she'd become used to it.

She stretched and yawned. And there was the cat from next door. Right there on her bed. How in the world had that cat gotten into thei— Chad's house?

She told the feline reprobate, "How'd you manage to get inside?" And in saying the words, she remembered the time-tested cat was skilled in darting through any closing door.

The cat yawned sleepily, and it was only then that Jo realized she was on the rim of the bed. The cat was in the middle. How like a male.

She told the cat, "Go home."

The cat turned his regal, orange-and-fawn-colored head and gave her a dismissively tolerant look. Then he rejected her and lay back to sleep again.

Being aligned along the side of the mattress, it was easy for Jo to get up. She just slid off the bed in a graceful, steady-footed move aside. The covers stayed under the cat with hardly a slip.

Jo took a shower, dressed and wandered down-stairs to the kitchen. She was feeling abandoned. Chad could have said goodbye to her first.

In leaving her asleep, he was being the male version of courtesy, consideration and compassion.

Yes. He was all of that. But he'd left her there alone in the silence. How familiar it was to her.

She went into the kitchen. In a bowl, she fixed some dry cereal with dried apricots, fig bits, pecans and grapes. She added milk and skipped the sugar. She poured a glass of milk and found the cat underfoot.

She considered the intruder and inquired, "Why don't you just go on home? Here. I'll open the door for you."

She went down the several steps to the back door and opened it. The cat sat down and regarded her as if she wasn't much of anything. He turned his head away and closed his eyes so that he wouldn't have to look at someone so stupid.

She gave him a bowl of milk.

As the cat deigned to lap it, Jo said, "There is a flaw in my genetics. First a user man and now a user cat. I need some serious help."

Having left his half boots on the mud pad by the front door, Chad walked silently into the kitchen and startled her by asking, "What sort of 'help' would you like?"

He kissed her in passing. Then he washed his hands and as he dried them on a towel, he observed her. "You don't look like a woman in distress."

She lowered her head so that she looked up at him big-eyed. Then she told Chad gently, "The cat refused to leave the house."

He gasped and put a very dramatic hand to his chest. "You want *me* to throw a little cat, like Old Yeller, out into the *snow* on a cold, winter morning in *January?*"

She put down her spoon and said, "I give up."

He rubbed his hands together and replied, "Good. Let's go upstairs and see if the mattress can take another go-around."

As she spoke, she turned her head forty different ways. "I'm eating."

"Eating comes before we do?"

She put her hand on her forehead and closed her eyes. Unfortunately, she smiled just the littlest bit.

He said superiorly, "I've gotcha."

But she corrected him. "No."

Six

Elsie, whom Jo called Else, came over the next day when Chad was in class. Else looked at her friend soberly and asked with honest reasoning, "Why are you here?"

Jo sighed and looked off into nothing as she replied, "Good question."

Elsie cautioned, "He isn't going to change. He's incapable."

"I know."

"Then why stir it all up again?" Elsie was so logical. "You are being uncommonly unkind to Chad."

Jo looked at her compassionate friend. She asked softly, "Am I so terrible?"

Elsie asked, "Are you?"

And Jo looked unseeing out the window for an anguished time before she closed her eyes down on her tears and replied softly, "Yes."

Elsie made no further comment, but she didn't move nor did she chide Jo any further.

The new tears slowly filled the bottoms of Jo's eyes. Slowly another one spilled over to run the path down her cheek. It was as if Jo didn't know the tears were forming or spilling. She didn't sniffle or gasp or move. She was separate from the tears.

Jo said in a low, controlled voice, "It was such a shock to see him again. I thought I was over him."

With honest compassion, Elsie asked, "How can you two be so close and yet poles apart?"

"We aren't when we're together."

"He has to make a living at something he loves as much as communicating premises, knowledge and facts."

"Yes."

Elsie's voice was gently earnest, "If you realize that, how can he teach in less time?"

"He can't."

There was another silence. The tears continued to pool and slowly spill to run down her cheek.

Elsie sniffled.

Jo turned her teared eyes to her friend and asked, "What's the matter?"

And in a shaky voice, her dear friend Elsie replied, "You." Then she rose in purpose and, saying nothing more, she left the house.

Others came to see Jo. Some were cool to her with the courtesy of alliance with Chad.

Some were just curious to see how Jo looked. To some there was no satisfaction, for Jo looked great. On top of that, she was mature and gracious. She was disgustingly smooth.

And she made some feel sour.

But there were her genuine acquaintances who were delighted to see her back again. They didn't know either Chad or her well enough to take sides. They were refreshingly neutral. They found her charmingly mature.

And of course, there were those who came eagerly to judge if the divorced pair was already sleeping together—again.

With a downstairs bath, there was no excuse for the snoopers to check out the sleeping arrangements. It would have done them no good to have gone upstairs. Even Chad's bedroom was again neat . . . for the cluttering papers were filed away. Natalie had seen to that.

By then, the hired three had just about accomplished their chore of filing. They were still working in his office, but the rest of the house had been freed. They'd done a remarkable job.

They'd even posted an index identifying where what was. Chad couldn't get over it.

Chad had not only paid them a bonus, but he'd had their profs over to view their work. Having been familiar with Chad's own "system," the tidier professors could not fail to be impressed.

Another of the visitors who came alone when Chad was in class was Peter Way. He was on the staff. He did not smile. He said to Jo, "I know Chad isn't here. May I come in?"

"Of course." Jo opened the door in some curiosity. She remembered Peter was an aloof, somber person. Jo had never had much communication with him.

She gestured to a chair and sat down on another. She asked, "How is Jeanne?"

Peter replied bitterly, "Jeanne took off just after you did."

"Oh?" Jo wasn't sure how to reply.

Peter was watching her with his head tilted back somewhat, and his face was frozen.

Jo thought: uh-oh. She said, "I'm sorry. We both know how difficult a separation can be."

"You did the same thing. Are you sorry about that, too?" And he was definitely hostile.

The hostility was so apparent that Jo replied, "I didn't know Jeanne was leaving you. I had my own problems."

Stiffly, Peter said harshly, "You seem to've gotten over your problems."

He was just a tad snide. His hostility was then obvious. Jo's voice was kind. "Chad and I are two different people from you and Jeanne. Our problems are ours, and yours are yours. I'm sorry you've had a rough time of it." She rose from her chair with ladylike grace. She smiled. "I'll tell Chad you came to visit. He'll be sorry to've missed you."

Peter retorted harshly, "He doesn't give a damn about me."

"Oh?" Jo frowned. Then she inquired bluntly, "What all have you done?"

"Probably about what he did to you."

"Peter, Chad is a good, lovable man—"

"Yeah, that's obvious."

"—and I left because I never saw him. He is a dedicated teacher. I'm selfish. I wanted Chad around. I loved him."

Peter's harsh voice altered her words. "You're a hot woman who needs sex."

She cautioned coldly, "Don't be too stupid. I have business to attend. I'm sorry to rush you off this way, but I really must call a customer."

He lolled in his chair and spread his knees. "What . . . sort of . . . customer?"

Standing straight with her hands loosely clasped in front of her, she replied, "Someone who bought the computer program for her business and isn't sure why it won't work. My company has people like me who lead people through those programs, and they find how simple they are."

"Want to lead me . . . through a program?"

She asked brusquely, "Do you have one of Phillips' programs?"

"No."

"Then I have no way of helping you. Peter, it's time for you to leave."

He watched Jo. "If you can come back here and crawl into bed with Chad, why not include me?"

She replied the obvious, "I don't love you."

"I can do anything he can."

"You—"

And the door opened as Trevor came inside. He stood silently, watching only the lolling man. He never gave Jo even a glance after seeing that she was standing by herself.

Peter eyed the young man distastefully with a scowl and said, "Run along." Then he said more vigorously, "Get out of here!"

Trevor replied, "Sorry, sir. I'm hired to mind the prof's house."

Peter looked sourly at Jo. "He's hired to service you, too?"

Jo said, "Peter. It's time for you to go."

Peter's voice cracked as he asked vulnerably, "You're discarding me, too?"

"I'm not in the circumstances to act in such a way."
She was maturely kind and logical. "Do leave."

"Send him off." Peter moved his head to indicate
Trevor.

"No. He's paid for the work he does for Chad. Go
along, Peter. Don't make it difficult for any of us."

Trevor still stood silently watching and listening.
While Trevor had moved aside so that the seated man
could leave easily, he was there.

Peter ignored the younger man. He said to Jo, "Go
with me."

"Of course not! Leave. Do that. I'll ask Chad to
contact you."

Peter's voice was ragged. "Did you get Jeanne to
leave me? Answer that."

"No." Jo replied quite calmly. "We didn't know
each other very well. She and I never discussed you or
her life with you. I'm as surprised as you must have
been."

"She just took off."

"If she left just after I did, it's been almost four
years. It's time for you to heal. Get some help. Go see
Oscar."

Peter slouched and was sour. "He gave up."

Jo said with gentle firmness, "You may not have
been ready to forgive Jeanne. You need help for
yourself. Go see Tina."

Peter scowled. "She's an old woman."

"She's also smart," Jo reminded Peter. "Listen to
her."

Peter looked sourly at the stern young man who was
still standing silently. He asked Trevor, "Don't you
have any other work to do?"

"No." Trevor didn't add the requisite "sir" to that.

Peter looked meanly at Jo. Then he slowly rose in such a way that Trevor shifted his feet. Peter gave the younger man a snide glance of bitter humor. Then he stood straight and looked at Jo.

Jo walked to the door and opened it. She said, "Goodbye."

And slowly, hesitantly, almost immovably, Peter did leave.

When he'd cleared the door and was on the porch, the front door closed solidly after him. Then Jo turned and saw that Trevor trembled, but he grinned at her.

She lifted a finger to her lips for his silence. Then she looked out of the door's glass fan window until Peter had walked down the driveway and to his car.

As Peter backed his car into the street, Trevor came from the back of the house. He'd locked the back door. He said to Jo, "You ought not invite strange men into your house. Didn't your mother ever tell you that?"

"What angel sent you here?"

Trevor laughed. "It was Chad."

"Why?"

"He wanted me to go over the file on the Etruscans. He told me not to chatter. So you tell him that when I came in here and found Peter hazing you that I didn't say one word." Then he frowned with his smile. "How could you be so cool with that guy? He was after you!"

Jo opened out her hands as she replied the obvious, "You were here."

Trevor loved it. "Give me a recommendation. Sign it. I'll carry it with me and it'll lull any female."

"You wouldn't push any woman."

He laughed. "No. You're right. I wouldn't." Then he told her, "But, Jo, you're sure a woman to protect. While you're older, you're something for a guy Chad's age. I just wonder if Chad didn't know Peter was coming over this way."

"There was no way he could," Jo said, "I was very lucky you came along when you did. Thank you."

"Do you think Peter would have really been that stupid with you?"

Jo shrugged. "I'm glad I didn't have to find out."

"Me, too."

While Jo hadn't planned to even mention the confrontation with Peter, Trevor obviously blabbed.

When his class was finished, Chad came home and walked in the door, pushing it closed with his foot as he called, "Jo!"

"I'm up here!"

"Is anyone with you?"

Even before she replied, "No," Trevor had already come out of the downstairs room and stood silently as Chad pierced the younger man with a look of ice.

While Jo was coming down the stairs, Trevor told Chad, "It's okay."

With lights shooting in his eyes, Chad snapped, "Then he was here?"

"Yeah."

Chad calmed himself and took a step before he asked Trevor, "Did he cause any problem?"

By then Jo had arrived and heard the question. "Thank you for sending Trevor over at that particular time."

"What happened?"

Jo shook her head once and said, "Nothing."

"He's always had the itch for you," Chad informed her. "What did he say to you?"

Jo shrugged, stalling, trying to think of a way to stall until Chad had settled down.

Very seriously, Trevor replied instead, "He was hassling her."

Trevor's confirmation made Chad's face blank. His head swung around as he looked at Jo. His eyes moved quickly on her to assess any harm and seeing no visible mark, he asked harshly, "Are you all right?"

Jo replied firmly, "Of course."

But Trevor replied, "I got here just at the right time, and it's a good thing you gave me a key. I didn't have to break anything to get in and—"

Jo said to Trevor, "Hush." Then she told Chad, "I had control."

Trevor made a male sound of disbelief.

Jo turned to the younger man and told him, "Don't make this any worse than it already is."

Chad snapped, "What's this 'worse' stuff?"

Jo asked Trevor, "Would you excuse us?" And she said it in a very kindly, formal manner that allowed him to leave with dignity.

However, he said to Chad, "You watch out for that scum."

And Jo's ex-husband told the dismissed young man, "Thanks."

Trevor nodded but while he went into the back room, he didn't close the door.

Chad went to Jo and took her arm into a very firm grasp and asked through his teeth, "Did Peter touch you?"

By then, Jo was a little ticked with male dominance. Did Chad think Peter was the first male hassler she'd coped with? She replied maturely, "No."

"Why was he here?"

She was still in control, therefore she was calm. "He thinks I talked Jeanne into leaving him because she left right after I did."

"Did you?"

Jo sighed. "I didn't know her well enough to discuss anything that sensitive. We were barely acquainted."

"What did he say to you?"

Instead of replying to his tense push, Jo told Chad, "Peter needs some help from Tina. He should go and talk to her. She would help him."

Chad snapped, "Why didn't you go to Tina, back then?"

"I couldn't change your life, Chad. You are as you are. You're a dedicated teacher."

"I can change."

"Oh, Chad. Don't even say it. Coming back here was another mistake. I need to go back to Chicago and leave you alone."

But he bitterly tasted the last word. "Alone."

"I'll know not to allow Peter inside again. It would have been all right, even if Trevor hadn't arrived as he did. I do admit I was glad to see him. But I've dealt with men before."

"Who?"

Jo looked impatiently at Chad. She frowned and worked her mouth. "You. Just lately."

"You feel as if you've 'dealt' with me?"

She grinned. "No choice at all."

He slowly, aggressively crowded her with his body. In a low voice that was intense, he asked, "What do you intend doing about me?"

She looked disgusted. "That again."

"Tell me."

She patted his shoulder kindly and explained gently, "It's just testosterone. As soon as you males allow us to geld you, we won't have this problem."

"Was he serious?"

She shrugged. "I didn't have to find out."

"I'll have a word with him."

"There's no need." She was firm. "With Trevor here, he had to leave. It won't happen again."

Chad regarded her. "I'm glad Trevor came when he did."

And she again admitted, "So was I."

It shouldn't have surprised Jo when, after that, she just about always had somebody underfoot. Well, they were mostly downstairs and she was upstairs, but when Chad wasn't home, someone was around. Several times it was Natalie.

Jo wondered how Natalie would respond if someone was after Chad's wife? Someone? Just Peter. But how much did Natalie's feelings for Chad influence her loyalty—for Jo?

Jo didn't want the premise tested.

However, it was with some serious regard that Jo considered the bitterness that was poisoning Peter. She found the opportunity to talk to Tina.

Tina advised Jo, "Don't be alone with Peter. I'll try talking to him. I know a good male shrink who might try getting the pus out of the wound of Peter's subconscious and—"

"Pus!" Jo was revolted.

Tina replied, "That's all it is. He's hurting, wounded. It's been too long. He's always been too quiet. We thought he was over the worst of it."

So Jo asked with real interest, "What could Jeanne have done differently?"

Tina shrugged. "Jeanne did what she should have. She left. The problem undoubtedly existed for some time before she left. The problem was the reason for her leaving.

"Peter's problem was more than likely there to begin with and none of Jeanne's doing. Peter is letting his life go more deeply sour and he needs help.

"I shall try to get him to do that. Not with me. It will take a man to help Peter. I don't believe any of us on staff here will be suitable. He's very private and more bitter than any of us realized. Your coming back and the triggering of his reaction gives us the awareness we didn't have. If he gets through this, it will be because of you."

Jo frowned at Tina and asked, "If you've known about Peter's bitterness, why haven't you—"

"We didn't know. He was courteously very quiet and aloof. He didn't change until you came back."

Jo asked, "What did my visiting Chad have to do with Peter?"

"His wife didn't come back. Chad's did. Peter's jealous."

"Men are a nuisance."

Tina shook her head slowly and smiled just a bit. "Life would be very dull without them."

* * *

Probably one of the more obvious ramifications of Peter's hostile visit was that Chad became more possessive of Jo. His lovemaking was different.

Their sexual encounters had always been well-done, but now it was beyond being simply skilled. He was more intense and much more possessive. It was the more explicit: I'm male, she's female and she's mine!

Men are, indeed, strange and basic.

Since Chad didn't feel the need to hit her over her head with a large club and drag her to his cave by the hair of her head, Jo could be amused by his attitude. And she was immeasurably thrilled by his lovemaking.

While we become more sophisticated and knowledgeable, all the basic instincts are still there.

Jo wondered who had thought up the bashing and dragging of women by men? Was it a cave joke? There isn't any evidence of such crass conduct. And Jo considered that most of what we assume is in error.

None of the long-ago skulls was cracked by clubs. Bones of Neanderthals were found in Germany. They'd been buried with garlands of flowers.

With the computer available, Jo's business life in Indianapolis became parallel to the way she worked in Chicago. She called one of her friends who had the keys to Jo's apartment.

Typically, Mickie was her own self. She responded, "So you're back with what's-his-face. How disgusting. What a mealymouthed, spineless rag doll you are!"

"I love you, too."

"I can't stand women who can't quite give up an unsuitable man. You're wasting your time. This will not look well on your marriageability survey. Get out of there and get back home!"

"I'll be in touch."

Mickie retorted, "See to it." And she hung up.

Sitting by the phone, with her hand still on it, Jo had to smile. Mickie was like Elsie. Elsie was more of a lady than Mickie, but both were staunch to the end. Their friendships were priceless.

Jo was fortunate in the women she knew. And she sat there, aware she was becoming homesick for Chicago. Chad had mesmerized her so that she hadn't realized how badly she missed her friends. She had just contacted almost all of them, all via her computer... Chad's computer.

How strange that she still automatically called Chad's house and belongings... hers.

Did he think of her apartment in Chicago as...his? He'd never mentioned possession. They *were* divorced. She'd been married to him for six years before they were divorced. A woman couldn't be faulted for feeling possessive of something after being around it for six years.

He'd had an Apple II Plus ten years ago. He hadn't updated that miracle until recently purchasing an Apple MacIntosh.

He hadn't had to support her in almost four years, so he could buy the new computer.

And she recalled the bank book still unclaimed on the bureau of what he called her room. He'd banked her "pin" money for almost four years. Fancy that.

Chad had told her he'd had no other woman since their divorce.

She'd lied and told him she'd had forty men, give or take a few.

She remembered the last night she was in their house. She'd fixed his favorite meal. Meat loaf, baked potatoes and string beans with a fruit salad. He'd only been thirty minutes late.

She had said, "Let's keep this easy. No recriminations, no regrets. This is a friendly farewell. I wish you well." She toasted him with her glass of wine. "I'll pay for the divorce."

They'd debated far into the night. He was hollow eyed and worn. She discarded the fact that he was suffering. She said, "The divorce is my responsibility."

He had shaken his head and opened his mouth to say something—

She had interrupted, "No. I have a job now, so the responsibility is mine. I'm the one who has chosen to leave."

She had then become earnest and communicating as a good friend. She had urged, "You need another woman who can do all the things you enjoy. One who can entertain herself . . . and one who can have children with you."

He had not replied. It had been too late.

Jo began to remember hilarious things that had happened along their way. The gaffes an eighteen-year-old bride can innocently perpetrate as a newlywed.

When she lightly starched his underwear and ironed them.

When she cut out and made his underwear, she sewed up the fly opening wrong. He never mentioned it to her but his friends all laughed hilariously and in convulsions. They'd had quite a bit of beer by then.

Jo had assumed it was the big purple polka dots. Chad loved purple and as underwear, it had seemed a discreet way for a professor to wear the color. Who would know?

Everybody on campus! He had told!

In that last evening, almost four years ago, Jo never mentioned how lonely she'd been. How lost. She'd been productively busy. She'd had plenty to do. She'd had friends and company. But she hadn't had Chad.

Her isolation had been from not seeing him enough.

And the night before she left, Chad had made poignant, exquisite love to her. She'd cried and his face was wet with his own tears. It was absolutely horrific, emotional turmoil.

They'd stirred in the next bleak morning. The sky had been abominably clear and the sun had been distastefully exuberant.

She was already packed. He had taken her to the train station. And the train was excruciatingly late. She'd told Chad, "Go on. I'm fine. This just stretches it all out insufferably."

"Come home."

And she'd cried.

She'd cried all the way to Chicago. A traveling salesman smiled and sat by her. *Here's a pigeon!* was clear on his face. He left after fifteen minutes of hearing way too much about a perfect man, some guy named Chad.

With her hand still on the phone in Chad's house, Jo sighed. Surely it would not all happen again? Surely she had more gumption than to repeat such a farce. She could visit her ex-husband and not get that emotionally involved. She could—couldn't she?

God could have done a better job on men. They were much too competitive. Look at Peter. He had no desire for Jo at *all*. His attention had come to her only because Chad's ex-wife was back and if she'd do Chad, why not him? It was totally testosterone. Men.

Without thinking about it, Jo made the meat loaf dinner for that evening. Chad was late again, but not too. Meat loaf is adaptable. However, she happened to glance at Chad when he saw what she was serving and his face went stark.

His head whipped to look at her and he asked tersely, "Are you leaving again?"

Surprised, Jo said, "Well, not yet. Why?"

He explained in a rasping, uneven voice, "You fed me this the last time you left me."

She looked at the meal in surprise. She'd just automatically made it after thinking about how she'd left the last time? And she subconsciously knew she'd leave again? How strange. She would leave.

Well, hell. She'd already known that. And so did Chad.

Soberly she observed his tense regard of her. She frowned at him. "You have to know that I will leave. We really aren't suited."

He jerked his chair out and sat down. "We'll talk about it later."

Uh-oh.

She sat more carefully. "If this visit has given you the feeling that I've moved back with you, you have to know you are mistaken."

He looked at her with a maturely serious and controlled gaze. He replied, "We'll see."

"Chad." She said it with mature tolerance. And she continued with adult reasoning of the obvious. "There's nothing to discuss. We are divorced."

His movements weren't smooth but they were dominant male. "We'll have another ceremony to reaffirm our vows."

She was somewhat annoyed and showed it by the narrowing of her eyelids. Quite gently, she reminded her ex-husband, "You know full well that it didn't work the last time. I was a chattel."

He became indignant. "Not even close. I sided with you and helped you expand. I must have gone too far. You've gone beyond me."

Impatiently annoyed, she retorted, "No one could possibly go 'beyond' you. You're a formidable teacher and a wonderful encourager."

His eyes pierced her. "But. There's the unspoken 'but' that dangles a criticism."

She smiled. "Arguing with you is really difficult. You smother me with logic."

"Then you agree that you are illogical?"

She finally spread her napkin on her lap and began to serve herself. "I agree that you are a clever debater. However, I know the land you claim so well. I can't live in such a desert."

Very seriously, he reminded her, "I've been here for supper every night. I've been here, with you, during the day."

She let it all go on by. She made no comment or protest. She delicately ate and was silent.

Chad lowered his chin and watched her from under his eyebrows. He was a formidably masculine man. She'd known that for some time. Years.

She appeared unruffled, as she continued to taste the food.

He had not yet begun to eat. The meal probably had a really bad memory for him. He needed to view his life with a more mature attitude.

He said, "When I told you to grow up, I didn't know you'd take the bull by the horns and go your own way."

She smiled at him.

He glowered.

Seven

It wasn't until their dinner had progressed silently to dessert that Chad mentioned, "We've been invited to the Head's house for a cocktail party on Friday."

Jo finished chewing and licked her lips before she blotted her mouth. She observed kindly, "One of my ancestors was a victim of the Spanish Inquisition. Will this be similar?"

"You are also and specifically invited. You will be my guest. There will be no beheadings nor shall you be dunked head down in boiling oil. The whole impulsive gathering is more than likely rampant curiosity... about you. However, this is almost the twenty-first century. People can accept a scarlet woman into their midst without undue reaction." He considered her with some censure. "Your suspicious cattish backlash does our hosts a disservice."

"I apologize."

He enunciated, "I shall accept your belated apology for them."

"How kind."

He squinted his eyes a trifle and questioned, "I don't believe I've ever inquired whether your family subjected you to any sort of discipline. Did they?"

She took a small spoonful of ice cream and lifted it to her mouth to close her lips around the treat. She smiled at Chad as she relished the discreet bit and then, again, she patted her lips with her napkin before she replied, "Not that I recall."

"That figures." He lifted his cup to his mouth.

She elaborated, "None was ever necessary. Any discipline would have been abuse of an innocent."

He barely covered his unbelieving, surprise expulsion of the sip into his quickly raised napkin.

She laughed with a closed mouth and dancing eyes.

He regarded her.

She moved her head and her body and licked her lips and smothered throat chuckles in a most ladylike and very prissy manner.

But that made him want to drag her off her chair, throw her over his shoulder and go up the stairs two at a time to their room and give her an intent physical dissertation on the duties of a female to a male.

However, being a civilized adult male, he continued rigorous self-discipline and regarded her with patience.

She moved in micro sassiness to indicate hilarious indifference. She didn't look at him. She did not actually smile. But the depths of her lip corners were suspect.

She busily ate another bit of ice cream. And as she did that, her eyelids raised and she looked at him across the table.

Chad was being unmovingly patient as he watched her.

It is always stimulating for a woman to be the sole interest of a male. Well...some males. Had it not been he but a stranger, a similar contemplation would have sent Jo right out of the room, up the stairs and locked in her bedroom.

It was only Chad's intense regard that stimulated her sex—her nipples, her stomach, the insides of her thighs. The undersides of her arms, her curled toes, her head, her mouth on which her lips were thickening, the surface of her skin— All of her.

He was exciting to her.

Why him?

Why *not* Peter? He was male. He had all the usual appendages. He was nice enough looking and intelligent. Why not Peter?

And she looked at Chad in a different way.

He shifted in his chair and asked, "What are you thinking...now?"

"Why do you ask?"

And her ex-husband explained, "You've changed."

That caught her attention. Did he know her that well? She asked, "How do you know?"

He explained, "You were being one way, and now you are another."

Curiosity impelled her to inquire, "What 'way' was I?"

"You were about to lead me to bed after you had teased me enough."

He was right. "So?"

"Now you're trying to figure out why?"

She nodded. "Close."

"What have I said that was 'close' to which way you're thinking?"

"I wondered why it was you, who could attract me to you, but no other man."

His mouth opened almost in anguish. His eyes squinted against the rush inside his body into his sex. His body curled a bit and his hands tensed.

She watched, sobered and wide-eyed. "Are you that susceptible?"

His voice was gravelly as he replied, "I am—to you."

"Wasn't it Benjamin Franklin who said all cats are gray after dark?"

Chad explained as any teacher does, "He was quoting. Most of his homilies were borrowed."

Disappointed, she replied, "I thought he was brilliant."

"I read a book which examined and traced his sources. People don't suddenly, individually become brilliant, they learn from someone else, many others or someone else's writings. His quotes were like the saying: Beware the young Turks. That goes back two thousand years."

"To the time of Christ?"

Chad explained, "Probably beyond that to the time of the beginning of man. There would be just another type of foreigner to beware about. Or another sect or businessman who could be clever."

"Taking your classes would be next on my agenda. You're fascinating."

He added, "And sexy."

"I don't believe there's ever been any question about that." She looked at him sorrowfully. "I just wish I could have had your babies."

His voice became a little hoarse with emotion. "Would babies have kept you here?"

"I would have had someone around."

"I was here." His voice was husky and gentle. "I wasn't away at war, or traveling or with any other woman."

"I needed to be productive somehow so I chose to be educated. I do appreciate that. You made it possible."

He soothed her. "Children grow up and move away."

"So do some empty wives."

"You were filled with life and my love."

She looked pensively at her fingers. Then sad eyes looked up at him. "The time I had with you wasn't enough." Before he could counter, she lifted her stopping hand and begged, "No more. Please. I just can't go on with all this. I can't go through the wringer again."

He was silent.

So was she.

Finally, although his voice was gruff with emotion, he asked, "Do you know to what sort of wringer you referred?"

"No." Her eyes were big and sad. Her face was still.

He supplied, "In olden days, women washed in big pots over fires outside. They used a pole to lift the boiled pieces from the water. They had to flap the cloths around to cool enough to take into their hands and wring them.

"The wringer was two close rounds that squeezed the water from the clothes. A man invented it to help women. Men are compassionate for women. The wringer was so efficient that men said that's what women did to them, too."

"Baloney," she retorted. "And no man figured out the wringer. Some women's hands hurt so that she got a man to help her. So *then* he solved the problem."

Chad told her, "You're very young. You're so worldly that I forget how young you are."

"It's called city shine." She quoted him who had used that as a need for her.

Chad had retrieved the saying from long ago. He instructed, "More recently it was for cowboys whose language was so crude that they were silent in mixed company."

Chad continued, "Cowboys were never tongue-tied. In polite society, they just couldn't trust the words that erupted from their mouths before their minds could censor what they said." He sighed with the burden. "Men have always had it rough with being around women."

Jo considered the male with whom she'd once found herself shackled. No matter which way or under what circumstances, Chad was a superior man.

How sad she'd never been able to have his babies. He was now thirty-eight. He needed another wife. Some nice, docile, fertile woman. Jo considered him. Who did she know who would be such a wife?

Any of them, but she rejected name after name, friend after friend, after friend. She became aware she was stingy. She would put her mind to it. There had to be a perfect woman for this perfect man.

Chad asked, "What on earth are you concentrating on so intensely?"

She smiled. "I might surprise you."

The dawn broke in his face and he grinned. "Okay."

"No. You don't understand. It is something else entirely. I've given you up. I've made my own life."

He soothed, "We'll take it a day at a time. No pressure."

No pressure? Pah! *No pressure!* He said that! Who did he think she was? Some village idiot?

Village idiot. She asked the history genius, "Why did every village have an idiot?"

He did blink as he restructured his thinking. He guessed, "A flawed but clever-tongued traveling salesman? Or perhaps he was the pot mender?"

"I knew you'd have an answer."

"No, no." He held up a modest, disclaiming hand. "A suggestion to be researched."

She bowed her head in acceptance of the professor's correction.

From there, they discussed the Etruscans. The flower children of a long, long-ago time. Those talented, gentle people who vanished, leaving statues whose curved lips smiled. There were those whose faces were not necessarily beautiful but were sculpted as sweetly human. They were of the first who built accessible houses, without walls. They trusted too well.

That started a discussion about houses and defense. There was the friendly sharing of lives. "The latch string is out." That allowed whoever came along to pull on the latch string and lift the inside, barricading bar to open the door inward.

And finally they watched a tape of a PBS presentation of how a castle was built. How clever. How amazing. It was a fortress.

But soon after it was built, there was invented the wooden catapult machines, which could be loaded with a fireball and the holding rope would be cut and throw the fire into the castle. The weapons of war. With each defense, there was soon a countering offense.

That was pretty much the way it would be for Jo if she was friendly with Chad. Her walls would be breached and her "fortune" taken away. Her fortune was her independent life. It was what she'd made of her life.

The only one to protect Jo, was Jo. And she would do that. Pretty soon. Not right then. He was still too vulnerable to her. She should teach him to reject her. She needed to free him of his sense of commitment to her.

She would.

It was bedtime. She would begin. She wouldn't go up the stairs with him like a willing sheep. She said, "I believe I'll go outside for a while. I haven't been out all day."

"It's too late for you to be walking tonight."

She smiled. "I'm a vulnerable castle?"

His reply was solemn. "Yes."

"I'll just be in the backyard. I need to breathe some fresh air."

"I'll go out with you."

She shook her head. "No. You go on and get ready for bed. It's late. I've kept you up much too long. I'll be fine."

He watched her with his eyes narrowed just the slightest bit, and his mouth moved to stubborn. He said, "I'll tap on the window when I'm finished in the bathroom."

She smiled. "Okay."

He said, "Good night."

She lifted her face for his kiss. It was not seductive or coaxing. His kiss was casual, quick. Just right.

He turned toward the stairs.

She went to the coat closet by the front door and pulled on her rough-hide, Marlboro boots. Next she wrapped a woolen scarf around her throat. She pulled on a flannel-lined, knitted stocking cap and a pair of heavy gloves. Then she pushed her arms into the sleeves of her coat, which had a zipped-in lining. That coat could cope with any weather.

She went out the side door and walked down the driveway to the rather limited backyard. The cold moon was out and the sky was clear with a billion twinkling stars. The bare limbs of the trees were subtle. Her breath frosted in the cold.

She breathed and looked around into the shadows. She turned her head and felt alive. It was late. The city's roar was muted almost to total silence by the lateness and the sound-absorbing snow. She picked up a double handful of snow and threw the ball at one of the young trees. The snow splattered.

She turned...and there stood...Chad? She asked, "Who—" And her voice was confident.

He said, "It's I. I believe we need to build a snowman."

She laughed. And they did just that. They got the first snowball so big, it wasn't plausible. However, it *could* be seen from inside the house.

So then they had to be clever on exactly which way to roll another snowball to get it big enough to be an acceptable body. And of course, they'd have to lift the snowball head even higher.

It took time and planning and work, and they grinned most of the time. It was fun.

For the snowman, Chad found a hat he'd been reluctantly planning to discard, and she donated her scarf. She was too warm by then, anyway. They had no coal to make the snowman's face.

In the kitchen, they found a carrot for a nose. They included dried prunes for the eyes and the buttons down the snowman's round stomach.

Finished, the pair stood back critically to evaluate their work. They immediately knew it was a masterpiece.

They went into the house and peeled off their coats and accoutrements. They went upstairs to her room, peeled off their clothes, got into bed and immediately became involved in another variety of exercise.

How could he be so skilled? How could he know just where on her hot, sweaty body she needed to be touched? How could such a tussle be so marvelously erotic? So different from their other lives?

His breaths were so hot. His lips and tongue scalded her flesh here and there...and there. In her heat, she shivered. Her moans of desire dribbled from her parted lips and her gasps were erotic.

How could such torment be so fantastic? How could the delay be so exquisite? How did he dare to do...that? And the relishing moan rode her breathy gasp.

At their passion's peak, how could their bodies actually leave the bed so that they floated in the universe? She saw all the planets and then the other suns. Which was theirs?

Who cared?

They rode the wild, brilliant space winds to their climax.

And they slowly drifted down and around in a leisurely way. They didn't worry about whether they'd land on their own planet, or some other. Or if they'd float into the middle of the city of New York, or maybe the desert out west.

Who cared?

Murmuring, smiling, sticky, replete, they finally settled down and went to sleep.

She dreamed she was pregnant. But even her dream was so impossible that she knew the doctor lied. And in her sleep, she wept in shivering breaths.

Chad wakened her. "What's the matter?"

"I—I don't know." She lied.

"You're probably hungry, and you remember the prunes on the snowman's fat belly."

Sadly, she nodded. "Probably."

He settled her against him, holding her, and he said in satisfaction, "You're just lucky you have me here to guard you from the bogeyman."

She never had nightmares. Never. But she heard her mouth reply sadly, "Yes."

His voice low and exceedingly tender, he said, "I think we ought to get married again."

She jerked in shock.

He laughed deep in his throat in that special laugh of a man with a woman. He said, "Surprised you, did I? That proves how sly and clever I can be. I promise that you'll never again be bored."

"I wasn't bored. I was alone."

There was some silence.

He reminded her, "I've been around enough since you came home."

She couldn't let it pass. He had to realize how it was. She told him gently, "I'm visiting, so you pay attention to me."

"You have used my computer for your business. You haven't been bored or alone. It's been a good balance."

So far. She didn't say the words. They were the first rebuttal. She considered them. She said, "This is only a visit. I'm not considering being married again."

He hugged her and his voice was low and soothing. "We'll take it a day at a time."

She was silent.

On Friday evening, they went to the formal cocktail party in which Jo had graciously been included. She was foot-dragging and uncomfortable about going. At a Keystone Crossing shop, she bought a dress that was discreet and clever. It wasn't red, but a nice subtle blackened tangerine.

She'd also purchased a pair of shoes with heels and soles but the rest was really only straps.

Chad in a tux was mind-blowing. Seeing him, any woman would have to have great control so that she wouldn't drag him into a corner under the drapes.

As usual, the women would gather around Chad and talk in high, animated voices to be sure of his attention; they would find reasons to touch him as they laughed and exclaimed.

Did she think that? Yeah. So she was possessive and jealous? They were divorced.

She'd hold on to the thought of not actually being his wife. She was only a guest at his house. She did not have the right to be jealous.

Jealous.

She was . . . jealous?

Had *that* been the basic problem? It hadn't been his ignoring her as much as it had been her jealousy that his attention wasn't always concentrated on her? Was she that narrow-minded?

Probably.

If it *was* so, she *had* been quite young. She was more mature now, and for one night, she could handle other women being drawn to Chad.

She'd scan their husbands and rattle the women. She'd been on her own for long enough that she could take care of herself. And she could see to it that she was involved in the conversations.

Well. Maybe.

In the last, almost four years in Chicago, the meetings she'd attended had been business meetings. The people had been strangers to one another and eager to share and learn. And flirt.

She'd never heard much sharing at the cocktail parties she'd attended in— Well, maybe it was because she hadn't known enough to even *listen* correctly. She'd learned a great deal about people and vocal exchange since she'd been in Chicago.

She could handle a cocktail party in Indy for one night.

Elsie loaned her a long, velvet coat to wear to the cocktail party. The coat had a matching round muff.

Chad responded to her questions as to who would be there, and who did what. Very few of the faculty would be there. With the knowledge, Jo was not exuberantly confident that she'd be able to manage any conversations at all.

And she remembered some of the ancient people who spoke of such old and dusty things that they'd been a dead bore to an outsider such as she.

Oh, well. The evening would end, eventually.

Time did pass.

And they did go to the cocktail party. With the snow a new inch thick after the walks had been cleared, Chad carried Jo from the car to the house door. He even stopped to greet other arrivers. The women's attentions were garnered by Chad's ease in standing there, holding Jo up off the snow.

She didn't weigh much.

But inside the house, the women were still talking about how Chad had carried Jo through the snow, and they had had to walk! That only made the men give Jo a good look over; and they agreed if they'd had the chance, they also would have carried her!

So Jo had the men's attentions. That wasn't good. However, it was not because she was bright and in business. It was because she was young and good-looking. And because her ex-husband had felt the need to carry her through the snow.

Men notice women who have the interest of another man. Especially if the man is no longer in charge of the woman.

So Jo spent the evening trying to talk to women and was interrupted by the men who wanted to talk to her. And Chad watched carefully and repeatedly moved between Jo and some other man who was touching Jo's arm or shoulder or back.

Chad irritated the liver out of Jo because she was skilled in taking care of herself. She...didn't need him anymore.

She replied to questions as another adult. She did not wiggle or flirt. She never had. She did not agree to anything stupid or unthought-out. She was herself. She had a good time.

Several women joined her and were equally staunch without being overbearing, and they were also courteous. None did any male bashing. And they adroitly avoided the deriding, chuffing, indulgent comments of some of the men.

As in some women who never allow a male to give an opinion, the male need to override other men and especially women is ingrained in some men. And there are men who are very, cripplingly indulgent.

It was wonderful for a woman to find men who respected what a female had to say and who responded as an equal. She'd had that amazing experience in Chicago, among the males her age, and she was used to it.

Also, she was not Chad's wife, and anything she did could not go against him for his "lack of control" over a wife.

It was fortunate that the climate at Butler had always been open and accepting. There, there hadn't been much of a problem.

And in the rest of society, it was prejudice in some quarters of males—and some females in the older generations—who still blocked women. That would pass...with their passing, with the diminishment of their power.

All of life was a struggle of some kind. The challenge made living more interesting.

With the evening ending, and in deeper snow, Chad carried Jo back to their car, and they drove to the restaurant, Norman's in the Caselton section of Indy. There they met others from the cocktail party and had dinner.

They returned home late and were lulled by good food, good company and stimulating conversation.

Chad got to carry Jo into the house. He put her down and said, "You owe me. I'll put the car away, and we can dicker on just what you owe."

"Let me guess."

As they lay in bed, silent, recovering, Jo asked, "Are you trying to catch up on the years since our divorce?"

His male voice was sleepy and contented. "I'm trying to lure you into believing I'm this potent." He yawned. "One of these days, I'll begin slacking off, exhausted, spent. But right now, I'm trying to pretend I'm this hot. It's been such a strain."

She chuckled in smothered laughter. "I've been trying to remember if you were this hungry before I left."

Sleepily emphatic, his speech was slow. "Oh, yes. It's just that, then, I was more considerate."

"Oh." And her throat chuckle was the intimate delight of a pleased woman.

So the days had gone on past, and Jo was still with Chad. She used his computer and contacted the tangled buyers of the various programs and led them through the web of knowledge. She made it simple. She was very good.

However, Chad was around the house less often. Jo was so busy that she didn't notice especially. That was probably because she no longer expected him to be there.

Chad gradually eased back into his old routine. It was what he chose. And he apparently thought she no longer needed him around all the time. Most of it. Some of the time.

The snow melted and the winds blew. The snowman stood alone. It was February. Her friends in Chicago were getting impatient with her. She'd sent her check for the rent of her apartment. She'd been forced to buy more clothing.

What was she doing there? Why was she delaying leaving?

Why didn't she just ... leave? Simply leave? Why would she continue to stay with Chad?

And it was then that she received the letter. It was anonymous. Of course. Such letters always are.

My dear,
I don't believe it's wise for you to stay with Chad, no longer married as you are.

I simply do not believe your conduct is a good example for the young people.

You must understand I am not trying to be censorious. I believe you need to consider your example and your influence on others.

A concerned friend

There was no way, at all, that Jo would show the letter to Chad. She used the fireplace to burn the letter not in anger, but in order to be positive the letter

wouldn't turn up and betray itself—and make Chad
defend her rights. It was then Jo realized he would.
She could not allow him to be censured for her conduct.

Even as Jo saw some truth in the letter, she was disgusted the writer chose to remain anonymous. Typed.
Was it a woman or was it a man who tried to appear
to write as a woman? Interesting.

What the letter indicated was true. People need to
conduct themselves with some discipline. Tacky people encouraged tacky conduct. Disruptive behavior
encouraged other disruption. The hidden writer did
have a point.

But the person did not allow Jo to know who chided
her.

How interesting that it wasn't the content of the
letter that annoyed Jo half as much as the writer hid-
ing cowardly in anonymity.

Or—

Did Jo actually care who had said the truth to her?

Eight

The anonymous letter had stirred a restless unease in Jo. While she really had no qualms at all in living openly with Chad, there was the niggling fact that someone besides her parents was monitoring her behavior.

She admitted to herself that her parents would not be pleased if they found out she was with Chad again. They loved Chad, but they would think her using him in this manner was selfish and unproductive.

Unproductive.

She was, she was.

But she wasn't a wife, either. And it had been she who had left him and divorced him.

So in the days that followed, Jo became more quiet. Chad didn't particularly notice because he had never considered her as chatty. She had never initiated a de-

bate. She responded to his visiting, and she contrib-
uted her own versions to his decisions.

That challenged him. He had to think deeper in order to counter her opinions.

It wasn't Chicago that had influenced her; she had
never been easily led or influenced.

Or so he thought.

However, after that anonymous note, Jo began to
withdraw. She spent time on the computer with her
friends in Chicago, or in leaving notes. She contacted
others with whom she was computer linked, and she
walked along the canal, fed the ducks and thought a
whole lot.

She wondered when the snowman had melted. She
retrieved Chad's hat from the yard and picked up her
scarf. It was all that was left of the snowman.

Just as before, those years ago, Chad didn't notice
Jo's increasing quietness. About half the time, Chad
made it home so that they ate supper together. They
slept together. They did talk. But she didn't confide in
him, and he was so distracted by his teaching that he
wasn't aware of her withdrawal.

He felt secure. He was satisfied that she was there
for him, and he didn't notice that she was not contented. She had not settled in.

Perhaps, since she'd been the same way years before, he thought she was being normal?

But the letter she'd received ate at Jo's sense of
fairness. She was delaying leaving Chad. She really
had no real plan for staying. However, she was still
there.

She needed to leave.

How vulgar to find a conscience had been lurking
beneath her active mind. To have it brought to the

surface by a rude elbow of an anonymous letter writer was even more diminishing.

One feels, when one is an adult, that one is in control. Isn't that true? And her droll subconscious replied, *One is!*

She groused to her subconscious that it hadn't needed to mock her with the "one" she'd just overused.

Her subconscious laughed.

That made Jo testy. She was one entity. How could a part of her be amused by her situation when she was suffering over it?

Was she . . . suffering?

Yeah.

Why?

Well, she was where she shouldn't be. She ought never to have come back to Indy with Chad. She should have resisted the temptation to be with him again. Clear back in the Dallas-Fort Worth airport, she should have shunned him, right away.

Of course.

Well, she could have had a polite soda with him and asked courteously how he was. She hadn't needed to reap the satisfaction of having all that time with him. She could have stopped it right off the bat.

—or anywhere along the way.

She should never have gone to the hotel with him. She should have resisted the temptation to taste him again and to selfishly have him all to herself.

She was having an attack of hindsight? It sure sounded that way.

What about Chad? Yeah. What about him?

What had all this time with her ex-husband gained for her? She was a greedy, unkind woman who was using a man she'd discarded. She was embarrassed to seem so loose and shunning of good conduct.

Grudgingly, she admitted it. She wasn't being kind to Chad. He loved her. He'd been true to her. He was just like he'd always been.

So she didn't love him . . . enough.

It wasn't that. It was the fact that she could not enhance his life. She couldn't . . . give . . . him anything to enrich his life. It would be better for her to leave.

Chad got home early. It was a day he'd carefully engineered—for Jo and himself. A surprise gift of time. They would have that day and the next all to themselves.

But he'd waited too long. She was gone.

There was a note on the pillow of his bed.

There is nothing to be gained in saying goodbye.
It was lovely to see you and be with you again.

But like anything that is flawed, there's no purpose in continuing half a life.

You are a wonderful man and a brilliant teacher.

My best wishes to you . . . forever.

Jo

She didn't put her last name. She figured he'd suspect which Jo had left the note.

Chad was zonked by the letter. It was a shocking surprise. As the days had been carefully passed, he'd just begun to breathe again. He'd thought she would stay.

He groaned and lifted back his head. His eyes teared and his whole soul was in agony. He could not believe that she'd done it again. She'd rejected him.

What was a man to do?

On the train back to Chicago, Jo was joined by a traveling salesman who had shouldered aside another man. The winner had settled down and spun out the entire tale of how sick he became on planes. How lonely it was to drive across long distances with just a radio.

She nodded here and there as the man continued his chatter. But she was lost in deep thought. Maybe it was depression? She felt she had reached a point that had broken off her marriage even more firmly than the divorce had done. But she didn't feel free so much as she felt alone.

Lost.

She reminded herself that she had never taken the time to grieve after she had divorced Chad those almost four years ago. She'd been too busy. She'd just sealed her grief for her marriage into some sort of time capsule and set it aside.

This last—it had been almost a month! A month! She had lingered all that time!

What business did she have to lollygag so carelessly around some man? And finally she wondered, how had it been for him to have her leave him... again?

In doing that, she had been careless and selfish.

With the added clothing she'd bought in Indy, Jo paid the porter to find her a cab. And some shadow man helped to load her things into the cab as he handed her a card.

Not recognizing her seatmate, Jo thought the man was some sort of railroad publicist.

She was so familiar with Chicago by then that she accepted its beauty areas and its potentially worked-on areas with the tolerance of a citizen.

At her destination, she found the cabdriver was a rooster man. He strutted. But he also had no trouble handling the boxes. She carried her sling suitcase.

She found the—was he a railroad publicist?—had paid for the cab.

It was just a good thing that her town house in Lincoln Park had an extra bedroom. With her purchases, she needed the additional closet space.

In a secluded, reclaimed area, her house was in one of the rows set on private, cobblestone streets, and all there were surrounded by high decorative iron fences. There were guarded entrances to the protected streets.

The fairly new buildings were in the style of turn-of-the-century town houses. There was a small garden opening out from her living room. That room had a high ceiling, with a ceiling fan to bring the heat down in winter. The upstairs hallway looked down on the living room.

She had a large-screen television, a VCR and a stereo with a CD player. There was central air and heat and a small fireplace. The floors were wooden. Her living room rug was a fine copy of an Oriental. It was pleasing to her eyes.

The Cabrini-Green public housing was about six blocks away. The papers discussed tearing down that housing area to make room for more expensive housing.

Jo didn't buy the newspaper of the area because only registered street people sold them, and they got only half of the money. She gave cash to begging people with some care.

She had no car and took cabs just about everywhere, in her business or to entertainment.

She was a Cubs fan.

She went on dates or out with girlfriends a good deal. She rarely grocery shopped. If she did, she went to a convenience store and paid well for prepared food like budget gourmet meals.

The Chicago entertainment potential is endless. She saw bands at bars on Clybourn Street and in west Lincoln Park. Occasionally she met friends in upscale coffeehouses to chat or maybe met others in a pub-type bar on Halsted Street.

She had a male friend who was a broker. His name was John Shaw. He was a serious person. But he could be amusing and easy to be around. And he liked her friends.

He had a new car. He'd chosen Japanese in order to avoid the BMW stereotype. It was four-door for business purposes and a conservative black. He was successful and financially quite comfortable.

Jo replied to a message given by her answering service, and John said, "I was about ready to go down to Indy and find you. Your notes on E-mail were very brief. I'll be over in twenty minutes."

That was a large surprise. John never left the office until five. It was only three-thirty.

Jo wasn't sure she wanted to face John at that time. She needed to be rested.

But he'd hung up the phone.

Her house was neat and orderly. The crew had been there only once since she'd left. That was all that had been needed.

She called her office contact and reported in as being available again. Sandra called back almost immediately. "Hi. Got a pencil?"

And she was given five places to do programming of computers ASAP. And she was given one person who needed help right away with a program.

Jo called each place of business and scheduled her arrival rather loosely for time. She only knew approximately how long each might take. With each she promised, "I'll call just before I come, to be sure it's a convenient time for you."

Then she activated her own computer as she called the last one who was wandering the extended maze inside his baffling computer.

The solution was simple. The man laughed. Jo took him through it two more times, and he was jubilant that it was so easy.

She went upstairs to stand in the hall overlooking the living room. She was pensive to be there. She hadn't unpacked.

She stood in the middle of a haze of inactivity. Her face was solemn. At a muffled distance, she heard John's car. She wasn't sure she wanted to see him. Not yet. She needed time to adjust to—being alone again.

Jo was firm. She and Chad were past history. Chad needed to be free of her. She would turn her back on him and create a new life. She never should have gone with him in TEXAS. She'd been a fool to cling—

She went back down the stairs, and John rang her doorbell. He had never before had to do that. She'd always opened the door as he'd come up the walk.

John wasn't as old as Chad. He was thirty. He grinned down at her and said, "My God, I didn't think you'd *ever* get back! Beth said you would come home. Your clothes were here."

"Hello, John." She smiled, but she stepped back before he could hug her.

Then John said, "You must be tired. I need to hug you and welcome you back to civilization. Is TEXAS what you thought it'd be?"

"Not exactly."

He grinned. "What'd you bring me?"

It was only then that she realized she'd bought him a gift on the island. It had to still be in her bag. She smiled a little sadly and said, "I haven't unpacked yet. You'll have to wait."

He took her against him and said in a very low voice, "I can wait for my gift, but I'd run out of patience with you gone this long. I've missed you."

How strange that such an aloof man would say something like that when they'd been only acquainted and comfortably casual. She didn't want such a complication. Not yet.

Not yet.

Ever again?

She laughed gently and released herself from John. "Slow day at the stock market?"

And even as John shrugged and shook his head, Jo thought how strange that she would chide John for giving her time when she'd left Chad for not being around.

She led the way to the little kitchen and put on the coffeepot.

Following, John took off his suit jacket and loosened his tie. John assured her, "I'm exceptionally good at unpacking. I can carry luggage upstairs. And you can tell me all of your adventures. Why did you stay away for so long? Did you take some classes?"

Reluctantly, she replied, "Sorta."

He continued to watch her. He was so interested and so pleased to be with her. "I really came over to protect you from all of your irritated friends who've been annoyed because you weren't here. Our arguments are flat without your fine logic."

She smiled in a faded way.

John observed her. "Are you that tired?"

She considered and replied, "Probably."

And in a low voice he asked seriously, "Are you all right?"

It was then that Jo realized she wasn't ready for John's concern or for his centering his attention on her.

She smiled a little and replied, "Just tired."

"I don't need the coffee. Let me carry your things upstairs. If I know your boss, you've already been given a sheaf of baffled computer people to baby."

Jo nodded one slow time. "You're right."

John regarded her. "You're really zonked. Let me help you get organized." And he immediately went to her luggage. "Does this go upstairs?" He grinned at her. "You've accumulated a bit more than you left with."

And she thought of going with Chad into Mexico. She said, "Yeah."

"You're really tired. We need to get you down for a nap."

Her smile was fragile. "No, I have some computer programming to do."

"Well . . ." He hesitated. Then he asked carefully, "How about my bringing supper over? We could just eat together, and I'll let you get to bed early."

What could she say? "Okay."

John stood looking at her. "I'm glad you're back. I— We've all missed you."

He was obviously very sensitive. He understood she was pulling back. She told him kindly, "I'm back. Shall I call Sylvia? Or Janet?"

Slowly, he agreed. "I'll pick up Ted and Rob."

"Fine."

It wasn't the conversation John had wanted. He was disappointed she had distanced herself.

She slid her arm through his as she walked him toward the door. He would leave and—

But he picked up her packages and cases, then he turned and carried them up the stairs asking, "Which room?"

"The one at the end."

She picked up the several leftover packages and followed him silently.

He put the things in her neat room, on her made bed. He mentioned, "It's always a surprise people make up their beds. Why do you?"

"I've been gone for a couple of weeks, and the cleaning crew has been here. They are chidingly tidy."

John grinned for the first time since his greeting. "Once I had a crew like that. Now I'm lucky if they clean the whole place each time."

"Come back for supper."

"I will. Shall I bring the women?"

"That would be nice. Otherwise they'll take a cab. Let me call them now to be sure they'll come over."

So he watched her as she called Sylvia and Janet at their places of work. Both women accepted easily, after they'd harangued her for being away for so long. Then she told them John would come by for them at their offices. His car was—

And both women had instantly replied, "Japanese and black."

"Of course."

When she hung up, John asked Jo, "Why did you say 'of course' after you told them I would pick them up?"

"No. It wasn't in response to you, it was to your automobile."

He was elaborately shocked. "My Japanese car is . . . an automobile?"

She was smooth and considerate. She asked in such a kind and concerned way, "Hadn't you known?"

"No. I thought it was just a . . . car."

"Baloney."

John loved it and laughed.

But Jo remembered Chad's reaction to her saying that word.

John went down to the living room while Jo changed her clothing. Then he drove her to the first place that needed her input for their recalcitrant computer.

John assumed he'd stay and watch, but she didn't even let him get out of the car. She smiled and thanked him and said, "I'll see you at my place for supper. Here's a key in case I'm not there yet."

Unfortunately, having Jo hand him her key gave John new hope.

Since he'd left his office early, John didn't feel comfortable going back to work so he simply went to

Jo's apartment, and he felt the thrill of unlocking her door.

Since the dining room was her home office, John set the table at the end of the living room and saw to the ice. He went to a flower shop and bought a bouquet. Then he bought a second one. He put one on the table and one over in the other end of the living room area.

He was pleased that she'd allowed him access to her house.

He called Ted and Rob and, like men everywhere, they preferred to be guests instead of figuring out what to eat by themselves. John told Sylvia and Janet to take cabs and he'd pay. They accepted that quite easily.

John was watching TV when Jo came home by cab. He got outside quickly enough, but she'd already paid the driver. They went back inside her place, and he was exquisitely aware they were together, but he also knew that other people were going to be there shortly.

He said, "Don't I get some kind of salute for setting the table?"

She looked and smiled. "The flowers are just beautiful! How nice to have them in this winter weather."

"The flowers are for you finally coming back home again. We've missed you. I have especially."

She smiled at him.

He said, "Welcome back."

She wasn't sure she could kiss him, so she pulled out her houndstooth woolen skirt and curtsied briefly. "Thank you, kind sir."

He came to her and put one arm around her. He looked at her and smoothed back her blond, winter-windblown hair. "I've missed you." He'd said it again. "You only sent one postcard," he scolded. "What kept you away for so long?"

"I went to Indy to see some old friends. I went to school there. My friend Else is there." And Chad. Her again discarded ex-husband.

He saw the gentle saddening of her face. Carefully, he asked, "Everybody okay?" He was trying to find out if the visited kin were hers.

"Fine."

He narrowed his eyes a tad. If they were "fine," why the sadness?

John offered to help Jo unpack, but she declined, "No, thank you. I'll do it later."

The guests arrived almost immediately. They were all acquainted. And they were used to one another. The invited guests brought additional guests and they were carrying Chinese. The neat table became cluttered with crowding foods, and people were sharing chairs.

The table's bouquet remained gorgeous. That collection of flowers was all that seemed to be elegant and controlled. The laughter and stories had to be repeated because there were too many conversations going at one time.

It was a good homecoming for Jo. They made her feel that she was back and among friends. She was a part of them.

John was inclined to linger, but he noted Jo's pale face and limp attitude. He hugged her, as did everybody else, and he took home a car full. The others took cabs.

* * *

Jo didn't unpack that night. She almost had to crawl up the stairs, her body and spirits were so overused. But she was grateful for her friends. Her thoughts clung to them so that she could avoid thinking about—him.

About not sleeping with—him. Of sleeping alone... again.

Before her TEXAS encounter with Chad, she'd been used to sleeping alone. With him in her bed, she hadn't thought even *once* about sleeping alone. He'd ruined her. Now she would again have to adjust to being alone.

Alone.

How could she think she was that alone when all those people had been in her house? They were true friends.

John could be a lover.

He was such a good man. He was perfect.

Why did Chad's image keep pushing against the wall she'd set up in her mind? He'd have to know, by now, she had left him. She had never given him her Chicago address or phone number. He'd been so sure she would stay that he hadn't bothered to ask for either one.

Or maybe he hadn't wanted to think of her leaving again. Therefore he hadn't called her attention to the fact that she lived somewhere else... not with him.

It was still early when Jo called Elsie and said to the sleep-wakened friend, "Don't you ever tell him where I am or how to get in touch with me."

A sleep-hazed Elsie grouched, "Oh, hell." And she hung up.

* * *

Jo took a long, hot shower. She stood there in the stream, reminding herself that she'd managed to be alone for almost four years and was doing very well before she saw him down in TEXAS.

Him? What him? Despairingly, Jo realized there was no other "him" who didn't have to be labeled. Her entire awareness knew that "him" was Chad Wilkins.

As the time passed, Jo apparently survived. She was occasionally aware that she was imbedded in grief. She'd never been the life of any party, but she'd been a contributor to the general conversations.

John treated her as if she'd been constructed of fragile glass. Her sad eyes watched him with regret. He was not her hus—ex-husband. But he was around. What a nice person John was. He was attentive and... there. And she added her rejection of John to her grieving.

Beth said to her, "What in hell's wrong with you? Have you seen a doctor? You're getting too skinny."

"Be quiet."

Even John asked, "Are you eating enough? You seem so..."

She supplied the word with some hostile impatience, "Skinny."

John shook his head. "I was thinking 'fragile' as a more descriptive word."

So her regard then of John was almost like grieving.

John asked softly, "What's the matter? I can fix anything."

She was honest. "I'm not right for you. You ought to look around."

John hesitated, then in a very kind manner, he lied. "We're friends. Friends are concerned about people in their groups. I'm concerned about you."

See? He was a superior, considerate man. He didn't burden her with his problems about her. He simply was there and concerned.

Actually, Jo was coping quite well. In a way. She was working and could do fantastic leading of baffled computerites who were so frustrated that they were ready to go back to books, letters, file cabinets and the phone.

And her relentless friends simply included her in whatever they were doing. She was never just left out. Nor was she abandoned. She was badgered, picked up, argued with and overridden. She had no real chance to withdraw from people or slide away into the doldrums.

Friends can be a real nuisance to a languishing mourner.

Nine

Among just about all mammal species there is recognizable grieving. And none of the species leaves a griever alone. Some animals know when a human is grieving. Dogs are particularly empathetic.

Jo had no dog.

But her friends just about exasperated her right out of her gourd! They never let up! It was all a great nuisance. They completely ignored her hostile rejection of their compassion.

They gave her no choice... at all!

They said, "Either you go or we stay. We'll be bored and sit around and sigh and roll our eyes and complain, but we will stay." It wasn't compassion; it was a threat.

So Jo would go along. It was a real irritation. She stubbornly saw nothing at the art exhibits and listened to nothing of the jazz group or the classic group.

During—whatever—she obstinately stayed sunk in her grieving.

She sighed and moved around in her seat in a non-disturbing, restless manner that indicated she was where she didn't want to be. It was the adult version of children's rebellion.

Kay told her, "You're a strong woman. We may very soon attack you and wring your neck."

She only gave Kay a surly, dismissive glance.

Jo lost herself in computer problems. That part of her mind worked perfectly. She retreated into that section and let the rotting rest of her life lie fallow.

Spring began. The jonquils and tulips burst forth. Then the spirea bushes flowered so gracefully and delicately. How could spring so easily approach and shut out the dreariness of winter? How rude of it. Without permission, it just came on.

Jo's group missed the Cubs' sold-out opening day. It was on the local channel as a treat, and they watched from Peggie's house. The rest watched. Jo didn't notice.

But there were other days. They all found time, and Jo was dragged to one of the first Cubs' home games. She was there. Surrounded by yelling, gluttonish people, wolfing hot dogs and all the other junk food. She was there, lost in her stupor.

Their yelling irritated Jo, and the sound of food being devoured was repugnant to her. She watched the movements of the players. She didn't keep track of the innings or who was winning the game. That's all it was, a game.

However, all along, and at the seventh-inning stretch, Jo had been dragged to her feet and she had woodenly sung along with Harry Caray. She'd done

that with each game. How can anyone refuse Harry
Caray's urging to help the Cubbies?

But Jo looked around at various times and wondered why she was where she was. The price of ad-
mission was wasted on her. She'd paid it.

Grudgingly, she finally admitted it was better to be
somewhere than to be home by herself in the silence.
Her acknowledgement of that was the first healing
step.

Then she began to taste the hot dogs. She'd been
eating them every game, but now she noticed and
asked for more mustard. She hadn't noticed food since
February.

Another time, she had a beer. It was the alcohol-free
type, and it still squinched her face. At least she tasted
it and did react.

After a while, at home, she turned on the stereo as
she had always done to fill the emptiness. Now, on
occasion, she heard the music. And there were those
wondrous opera stars who filled her soul and touched
inside her heart.

She knew she was recovering...enough. She understood she would never actually recover from Chad.
But she recognized that her life would go on. She
should be diligent in helping others so that her life
would have some purpose.

One day she noted and was a little surprised it was
already nearing the end of May. Time does pass. It
pays no attention to a grieving woman but just goes
blithely on its way.

That was probably a good thing.

Jo's attitude experienced a slow turnabout. Her life
was being altered so that she could survive her second
parting with Chad.

To herself, Jo called her ex-husband What's-his-name, in denial, but she held his real name close to her heart. There are stupid people who are that way and believe they're fooling themselves.

Eventually, Jo became aware of John, who was being very careful and patient with her.

That caused Jo to consider how to handle John. He ought not consider her. Or, uh, should she consider him?

Being sterile, she probably shouldn't take up any man's lifetime. She ought to look for a divorced man who already had children. John did not. Jo should leave him alone.

She thought she probably ought to find out if John wanted children. He was really a very kind and considerate man. *He* would be around. *John* wouldn't forget she was at home with supper on the table, waiting for him to show up.

John would call if he was delayed.

What's-his-name had never remembered. He'd come home surprised she was still up. He'd glance at the stove to say, "Oh, honey, I've already eaten."

She'd never actually hit him with the skillet, but she had been tempted. That was early in their marriage. Finally, finally, she hadn't waited. She'd eaten alone, cleared the table and gone to bed. It had been the logical, ordinary, natural thing to do.

When Jo's brain got to that point of remembering, she began to heal.

Her makeup was better. She walked with some verve. She paid more attention to her clothing. She even went shopping!

She bought a new dress.

She did not wear the things she'd bought in Mexico. She put those in the back of the guest room closet where she couldn't see them.

Why would she do that? She frowned. Well, she was sure no one in Chicago would be interested in such clothing or in the squeaky huaraches.

Actually, the clothing was unique and attractive, and if her friends saw them, they would immediately want the same things.

Jo understood that she had put the Mexico purchases in the back of the closet because they reminded her of that magic time with Chad. So. Why didn't she discard them? Any of her friends would be delighted to wear something that was unique.

She had no reply to the question. She just hid the Mexican things away so that she wouldn't see them.

But she would know they were there.

And she would remember the time spent with Chad, who was no longer her husband. Who was no longer around.

It had been she who had left him.

Yes.

Survival is a personal effort. No one should depend on others to get through grief. Each should straighten out his own life. The way she had. Sure.

By the end of May, Jo had given several suppers. It had been so long since she'd entertained that she was a little awkward handling the routine. She forgot to get cream and some of the coffee drinkers cheerfully groused because they'd had to add plain old milk to their coffee.

One thing about good friends, they have no compunction at all over criticizing a hostess. They opened doors and lifted lids and snooped openly. Not one of them had any discretion at all!

So it was a rainy June night that the group decided they'd just stay at Jo's and have supper there. No cabs were readily available, and only John had his car. They'd never all fit in it. And he kindly objected to ferrying them all back and forth in his car.

Jo's unexpected guests pitched in, snooping in her cupboards and her refrigerator as they pulled things out exclaiming, "This'll do." "Good gravy, my mother used to use this stuff!" and "Who'd ever believe a twenty-first century woman would have something like this in her fridge?"

Friends are a nuisance.

John was one of those who set the table. He took some pride in knowing where the dishes were and which silver to use. He even found the napkins. Those were in the ironing basket. John smoothed them out, folded them and placed them quite nicely on the table.

Jo observed him. Since her turnabout, she was aware of something beyond herself again. John was a natural-born helpmate. He would pitch in and help no matter the circumstances. He was bendable.

When John glanced up and caught her watching him, he smiled just the tiniest bit. He was then encouraged to share her attention and he was pleased.

Jo thought John looked confident. She lifted her chin just a tad and considered if she would allow him to be confident. Yeah. She would see whether or not she'd let that happen.

They were eating a strange assortment of frozen and saved desserts when the doorbell rang.

Pete groused, "It's probably Murray. He never knows when to go home. He'll probably want the rest of the ice cream. Tell him to run along home."

It was John who opened the door.

There stood a wet, laden man who lifted his eyebrows in some surprise. "Is this the Morris house?"

And rising from her chair in shock, not even seeing who it was but knowing that voice so well, Jo questioned, "Chad?"

Chad smiled across the silent room at his stunned ex-wife and replied, "Yes. May I come inside—out of the rain?"

How like Chad to intrude back into her life this way! And how was she supposed to say, *no!* to his intrusion? Who could turn anyone away on such a night?

Jo asked, "Whatever are you doing?"

He smiled his shrugging smile as a man does whose life is beyond his control. "I've taken a leave of absence and moved up here."

In stark horror, Jo said a guttural, "NO!"

"Yep. I have a close friend who is independent, and I've taken a chapter from her book. I'm going to write a very profound but titillating historical."

No one said a word.

There were several intakes of breaths. One male coughed in a throat-clearing way. John stood there as if he was guarding the gates. One of the women had told John that Jo's ex-husband had been named Chad.

Jo was still in shock. That was clear. She just stood there.

She was stunned.

How *dared* Chad to come into her house just when she was recovering from their last encounter?

It was the women who allowed Chad inside. The men all recognized Chad as the lethal male he was, and they stayed stilled and silent.

Beth was the only helpful one. She went to Chad. She told him, "I'm Beth Goodson. You're dripping wet. Let me have your coat. Your hat will be interesting when it dries! Here, Tim, move these over onto that rug. It can use some moisture."

Tim was slow to move. He glanced first at John. But John gave no indication of what Tim was to do.

Worse, Jo was immobilized.

So Bill got up and went to Chad. He asked, "You her ex?"

Chad didn't reply to that. He didn't want to seem a reject so soon. He smiled in his kind, to-a-new-student way and replied, "I'm Chad Wilkins." He held out his hand. He was probably the oldest man there.

People are automatically courteous to confident people. Bill replied, "I'm Bill Miller."

And easily, Chad commented, "I've heard Jo speak of you."

That made the frozen-with-shock Jo turn indignant. She never had even *mentioned* any of her friends to Chad! She had not ever! And how had he found out her address?

But ladies are made, not born, and she did as her momma had taught her. She was indignantly courteous to an intrusive guest.

With his luggage piled on the thirsty rug, which Beth had selected, Chad allowed his coat to be taken into the bathroom to drip in the tub. His floppy, wet hat was laid on the tiles by the door to the garden.

Another of the interested women handed Chad a drink, and he was included at the table. Her guests gave their names to the intruder.

Being a teacher, Chad remembered names. He flattered the women with a kindly, direct look—which saw them—as he was saying their names. His quiet behavior quietly challenged the men to get past their hostility.

Ensconced in her house, sitting at her table, Chad greeted his hostess with dancing eyes and a very slight, asinine smile.

She recognized the confident ease of him. How had he known where to find her? Had he deliberately chosen a wet, muggy day? Who could turn away any creature on such a night?

What she ought to do, right away, was to get him out of her house. She didn't know of any ladylike way of accomplishing that under those climatic circumstances.

When one's ex-husband, whom one had divorced—and has again discarded—turns up in that invasive manner, it's no surprise that one is indignant.

Her daddy was too far away for any help.

Actually, her dear father would very probably take Chad's side.

Why was Chad in Chicago with all that luggage? And she recalled that one piece of luggage had thudded just like it had down in TEXAS.

Chad stayed.

He stayed and stayed and stayed. There was no mention of him getting off to a hotel or motel or anything. He was there.

It was a very pleasant evening—for everyone else. Chad was clever with words and his humor was subtle and a delight. How vulgar he was to lure her friends into his fold.

She looked at the gathering to observe her guests all open and cordial to the stray who had arrived there and settled in.

She noted John was not fooled. He sat, leaned back, sober faced and watching.

Not counting Jo and John, everyone else had a good time.

Gradually, the guests began to tidy up and load the dishwasher. They moved about and got ready to leave. Chad saw them to the door. He was charming. How nasty of him.

John would have outstayed Chad, but Beth mentioned that she really had to get home. She had a big day coming up the next day. And it would begin too early.

As John quietly told Jo good-night, he asked, "Do you want me to come back?"

She was surprised and asked, "Tonight?"

"Yes." And John turned his eyes to look coldly over to Chad.

"Him? No. He's harmless. But thank you for being so thoughtful."

As soon as she said the words, she knew she was a fool. But what would she do if John did come back to her place? All three would sit and chat together? Chad wouldn't stay downstairs. He'd smile, excuse himself and go upstairs asking, "Which is my room?"

Jo told John, "He probably has some seminar here in Chicago. He won't be here long."

"Why can't he stay in a hotel?"

That surprised her. "On his income?"

And John said firmly, "I don't like his being here with you."

Jo replied, "He's no problem."

"I don't like the way he accepts that he's here."

That was an interesting observation. Chad had made himself right at home. How *had* he found out where she lived?

So John did leave, reluctantly. "I'll call you tomorrow."

She smiled and said, "Thank you."

Beth was already in John's car.

John didn't kiss Jo good-night. He was tempted to demonstrate that Jo was his, but Jo had never indicated she was. If John should kiss her, right then, she might pull back, and Chad might leap to her aid.

So John left. He was upset and tense and unhappy. However, riding in the car with Beth was soothing. She said all the right things.

So.

There they were, the no-longer-married couple, standing in her living room regarding each other.

Without giving her any opportunity to reject his being there, Chad said, "I've taken a sabbatical to write a book. A fictional historical. It's brilliant. Since I took you in while you were in school, I figured I might be able to stay here while I write."

"You could have done that back in Indy!"

"The kids would be knocking on my door to discuss things. I really will be better off away from campus." Then he smiled and added gently, "Turnabout is fair play."

Her mouth tasted sour. Turnabout. She'd thought the word meant she was getting over Chad. He took it to mean she'd support him while he worked on a book.

This was a complication she had never anticipated. Turnabout. Yeah. Sure. Having him around all the time? This wasn't a turnabout, it was a disaster!

He was saying, "If it's okay with you, I'll leave these wet things down here tonight and just take up the overnight case. Are we roomies?" He smiled.

"No."

His smile was tender.

She relaxed a bit and said, "You'll get the room at the top of the stairs." Then she added, "For now."

He smiled bigger.

She enunciated clearly, "We're not becoming a couple again. This is only temporary. I'll find you another place to stay."

She turned to the stairs as he picked up his overnight bag. She said, "I'll show you where the sheets are."

Following, he commented, "This is a bit different from TEXAS."

Not turning, she started up the stairs, but she retorted in an adult manner, "I'm older."

"But when you stayed with me, to go to school, you slept in my bed."

"Your bed was covered with unfiled papers."

Going up the stairs ahead of him, Jo's back was straight and prim. That didn't detract from her figure nor her grace. Chad smiled with tenderness.

She opened the linen closet in the hall and handed him a towel, sheets and pillowcases. She said, "These will do. The coverlet has been aired. It is not dusty."

He knew her housekeeping quite well and replied, "Your house is always spotless."

"The cleaning crew will appreciate the observation." Without saying a good-night, she stalked off down the hall to her room...and she closed her door.

As she was disrobing, he came through the bathroom and asked, "Any extra toothpaste?"

She'd forgotten the throughway through the bathroom. Clutching her slip to her chest, she gave him a dismissive look and replied, "In the cabinet."

He smiled wider and, behind his lashes, his eyes caught glints of light. "Any extra toothbrushes?"

"Use your finger."

She followed his movement back to the bathroom, but she took the doorknob, closed the bathroom door and locked it.

Then she had to go downstairs and use that bathroom. Men are such a nuisance.

Back upstairs, she took two aspirin and went to bed with a cold cloth on her forehead. The only stress she could enjoy was with computers. People tended to boggle her. Especially Chad.

She'd just gotten over the hump of missing him. How could he do this to her?

Any problem has a solution.

She would slide a woman into Chad's attention, and she'd be rid of him.

She went to sleep discarding women. How familiar.

When her alarm woke her up, Jo staggered out of her bed. Her mind was still whirling with tension-caused nightmares. She was absolutely stymied because the bathroom door refused to open. She stopped and frowned at it before she remembered why it was locked.

She carefully unlocked the door and cautiously opened it. The other door was closed. She went to lock it and found it was already locked!

Tit for tat?

She took a deep, adult breath to calm herself and turned on the shower. She stepped behind the curtain and was quiet, quick and very alert.

She finished in the bath and dressed in her locked room. Every second, she was conscious there was a man beyond the other door and he was Chad.

She went down the hall, carrying her shoes, and down the stairs on a wave of brain-injecting coffee fragrance.

Since Jo was so conscious of Chad sleeping in the room at the top of the stairs, she wasn't prepared for him to be in the kitchen, with breakfast almost ready.

"Good morning." He smiled at her. "Your Mexican purchases are in the back of my closet."

She looked at him. She would not mention that he would not be there long enough to call the closet "his." "I use it because no one stays with me more than a week."

Chad's mouth smiled too much and he had to put his hand up in the smoothing, whisker-feeling way men use to test their whiskers . . . or to hide smiles. He wasn't quick enough to hide the smile and anyway, his eyes twinkled.

He found this fiasco amusing? How nice—for him. She was not amused.

She looked at the set table and at the food he'd prepared. It looked just great, and she was hungry. In this time of stress, why did she have such an appetite?

She prissily ate a piece of toast, plain. And she had a glass of orange juice.

He did not object or chide her or anything. He did say, "No wonder you're so thin."

She did not respond.

He was pleasant and gave her the first section of the morning paper. He smiled as he did that and explained kindly, "I can read it later."

After a silent time, she refolded the shielding newspaper and finished her orange juice. She said, "Excuse me," automatically.

He grinned and replied, "You're excused."

She left the table feeling she was not in control of anything. Had Chad felt that way with her in his house? She'd had breakfast ready for him each morning.

She took a cab to her first assignment. The computer was really out of whack. It wasn't the computer, it was the users. Jo was just about five hours getting it all organized again and finding the misplaced files or lists. It was a challenge.

But being the person she was, she taught as she went along so that the users knew what they would be doing...the next time.

One person was very slow and was probably the reason for all the foul-ups. But the slowness wasn't ineptness. Whoever had taught or instructed that one had simply been too quick. Since the teacher knew what to do, he hadn't taken the time to be sure the learner was on the same track.

That happened quite a lot.

When Jo returned home by cab and saw Chad's car parked in front of her apartment, for one second, she was surprised to see it there. She hadn't had time to think of Chad being in Chicago.

He was there. He'd been there all the night before and all of that day.

Now what was she supposed to do?

Jo paid off the cabdriver and walked up to the door, and Chad opened it with an interested look.

Since he didn't say anything, she was hesitant to indicate he was there, in her house and she didn't know if he would leave. He'd said something about her taking care of him.

That was mind-boggling. To come home to Chad every day? How could she organize her life so that she would still be free?

Chad mentioned, "John came over."

That alarmed Jo. "Why?"

Chad chided, "You hadn't told him that you were with me that whole month."

Her lips thinned. "So you did."

"I'd thought he knew. He asked why I was here. And I told him I'm your husband."

"You are not! What did he say to that?"

Chad nodded in agreement with his words. "He said he didn't think he'd ever heard that you were still married."

"I'm not! What did John say?"

"Well, he was shocked. So I told him that you'd left me."

"What did you *mean* by telling him you're my husband?"

"I *was!* From the time you became an adult."

"So you do admit I'm adult? And I'm capable of deciding my own life?"

Very gently, Chad reminded her, "You've always done exactly what you wanted to do."

And she realized that was true.

Ten

It is something of a jolt for a woman, at twenty-eight, to realize at last that she is adult. Jo had always been self-determined. All the things Jo had done, had been done of her own free will.

The really shocking part of the premise was that Jo was responsible for her own actions, and she had been responsible for some long time. How rude of Chad to call it to her attention.

She told Chad with some censure, "You ought not be in my place. It isn't couth."

"In this day and age, people of opposite genders live together all the time, everywhere."

"Not in my family." She was blunt.

He inquired with polite interest, "Does that indicate that you've been brought up rather—differently?"

"More than likely."

Chad mentioned, "You just recently moved into my house and lived with me for over a month. Was that living with me . . . or was it—visiting?"

She said a nothing, "Yes." The word acknowledged the fact that she had stepped over her family's line. She was no different than he.

He was there as her guest. An uninvited one who had just indicated the convincing hammer of his own hospitality to her, which he held dangling over her head. Since he'd cared for her that month, she was obligated.

While she might feel rejecting . . . she *was* obligated.

Chad smiled nicely. "We'll just be sharing the apartment for a while."

"We are no longer married."

He licked his smile. "You want to get remarried?"

She flopped her arms in a very juvenile manner. "Good gravy!" But as she gave him a flashing glance of dismissal, her nose was breathing in the delicious aroma of something being cooked. Her mouth watered.

She had to lick her lips to keep from drooling as she said, "I trust that, from here on out, you will keep your observations and opinions and falsification of fact to yourself?"

He replied gravely, "Yes 'um."

She recognized that he was being cute. He expected her to grin and smooth things out between them. He was wrong.

He said, "I'm making your favorite baked pork chops and apples with onions for supper. Are you hungry?"

Her stomach growled in a shocking manner. She replied kindly, "It isn't quite supper time." She then turned and went off up the stairs to her room. Uninvited, her conscience considered her asinine behavior. She rejected she had been so stupidly awful.

Her conscience persisted.

She ignored it.

She changed into a new lounge outfit. A lighter color than her brown eyes, it was outrageously soft and slithery silk. She'd never had the guts to wear it before then. She didn't even hesitate to put it on. And she redid her makeup. She used a soft, natural lipstick, which coated her lips luminously.

She did that.

Chad had set their table near the French glass doors leading out onto the garden. The yard had been planted entirely with flowers that were perennials. They bloomed at different times, so there were always enough for a bouquet. No lawn. There was a circle of flagstones to step through the marvelous growth.

Chad commented, "I've never seen anything prettier."

She glanced up in surprise to find him looking out into the flowered growth beyond the glass doors.

She'd thought—

He continued, "Only you could have thought of such a perfect background for something as pretty as you."

She tilted her head, looked up and replied dismissively, "Balderdash."

He instantly grinned and his eyes were brimming with humor. He said, "I like that outfit. Why didn't you take it on our trip?"

"This is a lounge set, suitable to wear—alone—in one's house."

He wasn't put off. His grin softened and he replied, "Thank you."

She frowned. "Why do you . . . thank me? Because I've allowed you to stay overnight?"

"Because you've allowed me to see your body in that soft, salacious outfit."

She was shocked! She put her hand up high on her chest so that her breasts weren't covered and she gasped, "I wear this all the time!"

"Do you?" He carefully peeled a small sticker from the back of her sleeve and read it. "Wash with gentle soap. Do not dry-clean."

Jo's mother had told her from birth that she was never to lie. This proved it. She then dismissed the sticker. "I wonder what piece that was on. I've probably been sending something fragile to the cleaners."

He said one of his standbys, "Yes." But saying it was not an agreement with her comment. It only indicated the sticker was a confirmation of what he knew.

As he held her chair at the table, Jo thought it had never been wise to argue with Chad. She knew that. If anything indicated his theory was wrong, he admitted it with interest. His current "yes" meant only that he declined to argue with her.

That was because he wasn't yet sure how long she would let him stay.

Jo looked up at him as she finished chewing a succulent tidbit of pork and apple. She questioned with great care, which was too elaborately kind, "You do know I've rejected you?"

He was borderline elaborate with his astonishment as he dropped his fork clatteringly onto his plate. "No!"

She looked down as she raised her eyebrows. "We are not suited. I accept that."

In the kindest, gentlest voice, Chad replied, "You can accept that? Well, I cannot."

Jo looked up at him and studied him for a while. "In Indy, you readjusted to being yourself very well while I was around."

"I knew you were there. I knew if you needed me, I could be with you."

And she replied, "I take care of myself."

He ate slowly, silently. He offered no response.

She waited, eating distractedly. She finally said, "There's a Cubs game on the radio."

He looked up in some mild indignation. Then he said, "Do you want me to turn it on?"

"I thought you might want to hear it. The meal was wonderful. Thank you."

He smiled just a bit and only minimally nodded once.

She left the table, carrying her dishes into the kitchen. There, she rinsed them off into the garbage disposal and put the dishes into the dishwasher.

She went into her dining room office and closed the door. Jo had no work to actually do, right then, but she turned on the computer and went through the assigned people who needed computer help.

She contacted an urgent one. She figured the problem might be an hour's worth of time. However, the problem was simple. Even taking the client back over the process several times, the contact was finished in twenty minutes.

Jo was restless but didn't want to chat with Chad. It would seem too friendly. Via the computer, she left several messages around among her friends. Then she wrote a long letter to her parents. Her letters to them tended to be skeletons. This one was fully fleshed.

Jo didn't mention Chad in her letter. Not at all. She printed the letter and put it in an envelope. Her parents didn't use the computer linkup she'd given them. After three years, they were still adjusting to having the computer available.

The next morning, Chad again had breakfast ready for Jo when she came downstairs. It was cereal with four kinds of fresh fruits cut up over it. Why hadn't he shown he could cook when she had been with him?

So she asked him, "When did you learn to cook?"

"Since I was rudely abandoned."

She was skeptical. "You've learned to cook in just these last—five months?"

"The three something years after you divorced me."

"So you do recognize that it has now been almost four years since we were divorced."

He was smile-beginning surprised. "You remember the exact day?"

"It was the start of my freedom."

Jo accepted that Chad would be at her place only until he could find something suitable. Actually, he was already entrenched. He answered the phone and cheerfully took messages and he did note the calls. Even those from John.

Jo's friends included Chad without any fuss at all. John was quiet and watchful, but everyone else accepted Chad as if he was a part of the group.

Chad's friends hadn't been that forthcoming. Of course, they were somewhat older. Some were the age of Jo's grandparents. Perhaps that was why she had felt—different. Had her isolation been her own fault? She had felt young and immature so she had been withdrawn?

Surely not. Look how her younger-aged friends had accepted Chad!

Well, John hadn't. John had told just Jo. "I need to see you."

Beth heard and listened.

So when Jo and John met, the rest came along. They were their usual selves, mixing and separating into groups to remix. But they were always around.

So was Chad. How had he known where she and John would meet?

The next day, Jo went by cab from where she was working to meet what others in her group could make it to the Cubs game. John was there and shifted so that she could sit next to him.

He was careful of her. He turned his head and looked at her when her attention was elsewhere. She gave him every opportunity to watch her.

When the Cubs struck a player out or caught one off base, she laughed and shared the delight with John. They had the Wrigley Field fare for supper, and their conversations were casual and loosely shared. Then with the fifth inning, Chad showed up with—Beth!

Jo was awash in indignation. Indignation that Chad was with Beth? She had no reason. Why would she be indignant? She did not want another session with Chad. The indifferent Chad who did not treasure her. He nailed her down until he was sure of her, then he had gone off like a caveman—hunting. Only Chad's "hunting" was in reading the writings from long ago.

Down the row, the arriving couple moved in. Beth slid past both Jo and John and sat on the other side of John! That was pushy.

But Chad sat next to Jo.

Why was her body so exquisitely conscious of his? Why was she controlling her breathing? Why were her movements so stiff and jerky?

She was indignant.

Well. Of course!

How could Chad weasel his way into her group through Beth? Why... Beth?

Jo turned to say something to John, but Beth was talking to John. And John was listening. John did not instantly realize Jo wanted his attention.

The game was soon over, and the Cubs lost. The group agreed to meet at an upscale pub-type bar on Halsted street. It took two and a half cabs to get them over there.

They rarely left the northside loop except on business or when they traveled.

And again, John took Beth and Chad along when they went home. Beth lived six blocks from John. He dropped Chad off along with Jo.

It was like being half of a couple. She deliberately kissed John good-night. Beth didn't watch, but Chad stood on the walkway and stonily observed.

When they got inside her place, Chad took his handkerchief and said, "Here."

Jo looked at him, not knowing what he meant.

So Chad wiped her mouth just a tad harshly. Then he kissed her the double-whammy, woman-killer kiss Jo hadn't had in some time.

He leaned the ruined woman against the wall and went off upstairs.

How rude of him.

It took her some concentrated time to get herself oriented and organized so that she also could climb the tricky stairs and go to her room. She passed Chad's closed door and could hear nothing.

In her room, she tapped on her locked bathroom door and received no response, so she opened it to find the other door closed. Somewhat mesmerized, she silently turned that knob, but the door was locked.

She went to bed to dream lascivious dreams in which a passionately attentive John turned into Chad who laughed uproariously. She was shocked.

How could Jo possibly gain weight during such a stressful time? Her body wasn't still bony but was smoothing out and subtly rounding. Her clothes fit better.

She decided she was eating because she was so distressed, over Chad living there with her, that she was off kilter.

However, *not* eating had been because she was off kilter. How could—?

Never mind!

She worked and the summer continued. Chad was still entrenched. He said he couldn't find a place. Beth was helping him search for the right place.

Beth? Was that hussy trying to get her fingernails into... Chad? How vulgar of her.

Actually, Chad's and Jo's relationship was very like it had been when they were married. Except for the sex.

No sex.

She avoided touching him.

She went to great pains not to touch him. That was easy because she always knew exactly where he was.

When they were meeting in one of the doorways or in a narrow part of the kitchen, Jo would stop and pull back, standing straight and pulling in her...stomach. That left her breasts jutting out obviously.

He'd smile.

But he didn't stand aside and allow her to go first. He just went on slowly past, his eyelashes down, covering his eyes as he sought his steps.

That's what she thought he was watching.

The whole situation was simply ridiculous, Jo told herself as she would sit back from some computer. One that was misbehaving because some person had been briefly stupid... or distracted?

Her hours were long and she was late at some of her group's doings. Chad was always there.

He'd been in her house for weeks. By then he was considered a Chicago native. It takes a while to be recognized as a Chicago native. In TEXAS, one is a native as soon as one's feet touches the soil.

Maybe the difference is that Chicago is a large city. That was not in TEXAS-like attitude but in actual population count.

Gradually, Jo became accustomed to having Chad around. She reminded herself of the fact that they were no longer married. He lured her into conversations. He mentioned the passage of time spent together.

He asked her to go out to supper with him. "I've found a new place just opened. It's called Cherir. They cherish their patrons."

Jo eyed him suspiciously before she replied, "Okay."

She went off to program a computer and was a little longer than she'd planned. That was mostly because she'd told the office manager that she had to make a call. It was an emergency.

She went to a phone booth and called all her uncommitted friends. Then she called Cherir.

So when Chad arrived a tad early, carrying a discreet bouquet, he did blink at the size of the Chad

Wilkins reserved table. He questioned discreetly, and was informed of the number who were to attend.

Chad had no idea who all would arrive. The only thing he could do, and which he did, was to set cards to indicate "male" and "female." Jo would sit next to him.

Jo was the last to arrive. Had that been deliberate? She wove her way through the elegant little restaurant, which was jammed, and came to the table.

She was greeted and two women were complaining that they were "men" for the evening. There were more women there than men. Generally it was the other way around.

Outside of claiming they were "men," the two women talked in husky voices and said outrageous things and mentioned all the legal sports. One bought a cigar and put it into her mouth still wrapped.

What was the difference? How about the men dressed as women in the TV Bud commercials? However, neither of their evening's designated "men" used the men's john.

It was a hilarious evening. Jo exchanged seats with other guests around the whole table and hardly sat by Chad at all.

Chad's tolerance was ingrained. He was amused and patient. How can men be that way? A woman would have been crushed, indifferent or furious.

Men are strange.

John took Jo home, and he kissed her good-night. It was a hungry, passionate kiss. Jo was shocked. He was forward. She slid away from John and found the door unlocked. She smiled up at John and said a sisterly, "Good night."

She went inside and closed the door, leaning against it as she locked the bolt. She realized she not only didn't but she *couldn't* love John.

The realization made her gloomy. She was doomed to an empty life. She couldn't marry anyone else. She was cured of marriage. She gave up. She would be an old mai— She would remain single.

She drooped upstairs to her room at the end of the hall that looked down onto the living room. And she recognized that she would come home exactly this way all the rest of her life.

Jo's constant companions would be computers. Ailing ones.

On her pillow was the charming bouquet Chad had put by her plate at Cherir's.

Tears leaked.

She got ready for bed in a distracted wave of seeing into the future and looking back. How dare Chad do something so charming?

It was courting behavior. Jo knew it well.

She also knew the conduct of men who married and, having won the bride, ignored the wife.

Jo didn't rush through the bathroom doors to Chad to thank him for the bouquet. She moved thoughtfully and slowly to undress. Without brushing her teeth, for the first time in not quite her entire twenty-eight years, Jo stripped naked and crawled into her chaste bed.

She considered her life. And she realized that Chad had gradually ignored her and taken her for granted when she stayed with him and wasn't married to him. It wasn't marriage, it was being secure that made a man careless?

What about all the men whose lives were dedicated to good deeds, to government, to research, to defending the fort, the country and our fragile world?

Or to teaching those coming into responsibility? Were they selfish?

Jo went to sleep dreaming of Napoleon in a tent on a battlefield, furiously writing jealous letters to Josephine.

Jo seemed in a vacuum of contemplation. Chad observed her going to the pantry and standing in the door, not moving.

He questioned, "Jo?"

And she turned blank faced and didn't actually see him. "Ummm?"

"Are you all right?"

She moved a hand out as if to unsettle a lazy fly. "Just thinking."

And Chad was left to speculate on what she might be thinking. He walked a lot during that time. He learned the city quite well.

The time went toward fall. When Jo opened the door, she knew a man lived there in her house. It had an aroma of male. Only then did she vaguely remember coming into the house to a light fragrance. Female.

Her house had become a man's.

How strange to realize she would miss the smell of Chad if he left. For the first time, she asked, "How's the book coming?"

Chad eyed her. If he admitted it was finished, would she suggest he leave? He didn't tell her it had been sent to a publishing house; he replied, "Okay."

She nodded slowly, still distracted.

He asked, "Are you all right?"

She looked at him in surprise. She replied, "Yes," in some puzzlement.

Once when she came home after finally solving a computer's loused-up behavior, she was startled to see Chad in her house. She was obviously surprised he was there.

Had she been thinking of John? Chad's stomach clenched as he watched her soberly. He asked with some anguish, "Am I that easy to forget?"

And she asked, "Hmm?"

That really rattled him. He told her, "I'm your husband, I ache for you. Let me hold you."

She watched him with something like grief. "This is how it was each beginning. You were hungry for a woman, and you convinced me it would be that way all our lives. Let me go."

She went dragging off up the stairs. Chad stood there by the front door and listened as the faint sound of the shower could be heard.

He groaned to be the water washing over her body. He would touch her face so gently. Then he would run slowly down her throat, over her breasts and stomach and down her thighs.

Chad put his face into his hands and suffered.

He was hollow-eyed, sexually on his ear and defeated. He understood clearly that it had been too long. She was immune to him.

He'd lost.

What was he to do?

Defeated and knowing it, Chad used the next gathering at Jo's as an excuse to tell John, "You leave my wife alone."

Was John rattled? No. He replied with some civilized challenge and discarded such a labeling, "She is no longer your wife."

"I'm here." How could two words carry such a range of supposition? Chad's eyes glinted. Let John figure it out. Just the two words implied he was sleeping with Jo.

When the party had ended, Beth went out to John's car while John said good-night to Jo.

Chad watched from the shadow of his bedroom door down to the entrance where the couple stood.

John took Jo into his arms.

Even to Chad's pain-narrowed eyes, Jo simply allowed it. Her hands were on John's arms, not around his neck.

John gathered Jo close and one of his hands went down her spine to pull her close to his body! Chad gasped with the pain that hit in him.

And John's kiss was spectacular...

But Chad witnessed the soberingly remarkable fact that Jo didn't get rattled by John's kiss.

Not the way she had with him. It was only then that Chad realized Jo didn't love John! Chad smiled. She was his! Well, maybe not. But she sure wasn't John's, either.

John left. He was gone. Jo came up the stairs. Yet again, Chad had room to work to convince her they were made for each other. So the next day he began his sales pitch. "We are well suited. Since I no longer teach, we have your mounting bank balance in Indy, and we can travel. I can contribute my share to the pot. Alone, I've been very frugal. How about just going around and about?"

She shook her head. But she'd looked up in surprise first.

He brought home brochures and spread them around. She was lured. But she claimed that she had too many computers lined up to handle.

Actually, she was one of a crew and anyone could handle what she did. The others of the crew could fill the gap if she wasn't there.

Chad knew that.

He said, "Come back to me. I love you."

As usual, she scoffed. "For a while? You just want me in the house/barrel with a lid on it so that I'm there when you have the time."

He shook his head. "At the Dallas-Fort Worth airport, I couldn't believe you were really there and I had another chance with you."

Sadly, she said, "We've tried twice. It just doesn't work. You're at a crossroads and have the time to look around again. That's all it is."

"Third time charm." He lured her to try.

"That's an old wives' tale. It's nice to have those to dust off on occasion. None of them is true. Permanence between us becomes indifference on your part."

However, they went to a Cubs game and it was so tight that the crowd and the separated couple, who were sitting together, were riveted. As riveted as one is at a tense baseball game.

They were exuberant! They yelled and did the wave, and ate everything and were very animated. It was exhausting.

At the last of the eleventh inning, the Cubs won! THE CUBS WON! Jo threw her arms around Chad and hugged him! Chad!

He groaned and his arms slid around her in rigid pleasure.

To Jo, it just felt so good. She made sounds in gasps. She was in the midst of a maelstrom of sound that was Cubs' fans yelling in victory. She wasn't being much different from a whole lot of joyous people so she could relish the moment of being back in Chad's arms.

She opened her eyes in all that hoopla, and her vision met the amused regard of... Beth. John wasn't there. He'd had a client he couldn't refuse. But Beth was, and she saw Jo and Chad.

Jo raised her eyebrows as she grinned and she shrugged.

Beth laughed out loud.

As the slow, noisy, celebrating fans finally exited past the patient Cub monitors, Jo was holding Chad's hand and Beth was momentarily next to her. Jo said, "What'll I do about John?"

Beth grinned. "I'll think of something."

So as they were separated from the rest of their group, by Chad, Jo mentioned to him, "Beth loves John."

And Chad replied, "I know."

"How did you know that?"

He looked at Jo and replied gently, "I know that you love me."

Jo frowned and walked along considering Chad's words. It was probably true. She did love Chad. More than likely, she always would. Maybe romance was the pepper seasoning on responsibility? Could be.

Chad took her to a strange, new restaurant. It was out of their usual area. And it was very nice.

He consulted her over the menu, and she had no idea at what she was nibbling as they flirted just like newly met people. That amused them both.

She'd been punishing him... deliberately? It had been juvenile of her. How tolerant and patient he was.

She asked him quite seriously, "Are you sure you want to waste more time with me? You really ought to have babies."

"I'm mentally unsuited for anything like that. The world is overpopulated now. I want you for the rest of my life."

"Are you going back to teaching?"

"I doubt it. I like cooking and writing." He sipped his wine before he added, "I may do a cookbook of ancient times."

"You could add the recipes as you go along in your text about the times and trials of whenever."

He considered. "I could."

"Why not?"

Then he set a scene of tension for an ailing commander of a spearsman corps. And he told what all they ate.

She suggested, "You may have to update the words so readers will know what you're saying."

"I'll consult with you."

"In another time, making . . . Love . . . would be the same, wouldn't it?"

He lifted his glass of wine. Before he sipped it, he said, "And Jealousy."

"I've been awful."

"No." His voice was very gentle. "You needed to catch my attention. You did. I find I want you more than I want anything else."

"I suppose when I say that you ought to go back to teaching, you'll think I'm crazy?"

He nodded. "Probably."

"But you should teach. I know now that you really love me. I never understood that before now."

His smile was a benediction.

"You do realize we've been divorced for over four years?"

So he inquired with a slight smile, "How do you know?"

She began to speak and then grinned. "So I kept count."

"Exactly. That's all that's kept my hope alive."

They spoke then of many things they had shared. They spoke of people, and he mentioned some really brilliant students.

Jo listened. She added ideas of her own. She could do that now. She slowly realized she had grown up and she felt a partner to Chad. She was equally involved with the world. She was adult. How strange she realized that . . . finally.

At one point, when he took her hand in his, she gently scratched her fingernails on his susceptible palm. How blatant. And while she knew she wanted him, then, she would keep him for the rest of her life.

When they returned to her place, Chad said, "Let's have a nightcap."

She agreed, and they sat in the living room with their slowly sipped wine.

He went upstairs as she tidied the kitchen. He took the Mexican toad purse and put it on one of her pillows.

When Jo came into her room, she was surprised that he was in his own room. Then she saw the Mexican toad purse in her bed. She considered it a minute and her smile was fond.

She went into the bathroom and when she came back into her room, the lights were out. She considered. Then she just went on over and lifted back the covers and slid naked into her bed.

The toad was first. She touched it. But then it was Chad whom she touched.

"I'm really a prince. Love me and I'll be one for you."

She sighed, "You'll probably give me warts."

* * * * *

SILHOUETTE®
Desire®

COMING NEXT MONTH

#979 MEGAN'S MARRIAGE—Annette Broadrick
Daughters of Texas
February's *Man of the Month* and Aqua Verde County's most eligible bachelor, Travis Hanes, wanted Megan O'Brien as his bride. And now that she needed his help, could Travis finally talk stubborn Megan into being the wife he wanted?

#980 ASSIGNMENT: MARRIAGE—Jackie Merritt
Tuck Hannigan had to pose as pretty Nicole Currie's husband if he was going to protect her. Could this phony marriage get the confirmed bachelor thinking about a honyemoon for real?

#981 REESE: THE UNTAMED—Susan Connell
Sons and Lovers
Notorious playboy Reese Marchand knew mysteriously sexy Beth Langdon was trouble. But he couldn't stay away from the long-legged beauty—even if it meant revealing his long-kept secret.

#982 THIS IS MY CHILD—Lucy Gordon
Single dad Giles Haverill was the only man who could help Melanie Haynes find the baby she'd been forced to give up years ago. Unfortunately, he was also the one man she could never love....

#983 DADDY'S CHOICE—Doreen Owens Malek
Taylor Kirkland's goal in life was to regain custody of his daughter. But then he met Carol Lansing—an irresistible woman whose love could cost him that dream....

#984 HUSBAND MATERIAL—Rita Rainville
Matthew Flint never thought he would make a good husband—until he lost the only woman he ever loved. Now he would do anything to convince Libby Cassidy he really was husband material.

Take 4 bestselling love stories FREE

Plus get a FREE surprise gift!

Special Limited-time Offer

Mail to Silhouette Reader Service™

3010 Walden Avenue
P.O. Box 1867
Buffalo, N.Y. 14269-1867

YES! Please send me 4 free Silhouette Desire® novels and my free surprise gift. Then send me 6 brand-new novels every month, which I will receive months before they appear in bookstores. Bill me at the low price of $2.66 each plus 25¢ delivery and applicable sales tax, if any.* That's the complete price and a savings of over 10% off the cover prices—quite a bargain! I understand that accepting the books and gift places me under no obligation ever to buy any books. I can always return a shipment and cancel at any time. Even if I never buy another book from Silhouette, the 4 free books and the surprise gift are mine to keep forever.

225 BPA AWPN

Name _____ (PLEASE PRINT)

Address _____ Apt. No. _____

City _____ State _____ Zip _____

This offer is limited to one order per household and not valid to present Silhouette Desire® subscribers. *Terms and prices are subject to change without notice.
Sales tax applicable in N.Y.

UDES-995   ©1990 Harlequin Enterprises Limited

Are your lips succulent, impetuous, delicious or racy?

Find out in a very special Valentine's Day promotion—THAT SPECIAL KISS!

Inside four special Harlequin and Silhouette February books are details for THAT SPECIAL KISS! explaining how you can have your lip prints read by a romance expert.

Look for details in the following series books, written by four of Harlequin and Silhouette readers' favorite authors:

Silhouette Intimate Moments #691
Mackenzie's Pleasure by *New York Times* bestselling author Linda Howard

Harlequin Romance #3395
Because of the Baby by Debbie Macomber

Silhouette Desire #979
Megan's Marriage by Annette Broadrick

Harlequin Presents #1793
The One and Only by Carole Mortimer

Fun, romance, four top-selling authors, plus a **FREE** gift! This is a very special Valentine's Day you won't want to miss! Only from Harlequin and Silhouette.

VAL96

They're the hardest working, sexiest women in the Lone Star State...they're

Annette Broadrick

The O'Brien sisters: Megan, Mollie and Maribeth. Meet them and the men who want to capture their hearts in these titles from Annette Broadrick:

MEGAN'S MARRIAGE
(February, Silhouette Desire #979)

The *MAN OF THE MONTH* is getting married to *very* reluctant bride Megan O'Brien!

INSTANT MOMMY
(March, Silhouette Romance #1139)

A *BUNDLE OF JOY* brings Mollie O'Brien together with the man she's always loved.

THE GROOM, I PRESUME?
(April, Silhouette Desire #992)

Maribeth O'Brien's been left at the altar—but this bride won't have to wait long for wedding bells to ring!

Don't miss the DAUGHTERS OF TEXAS—three brides waiting to lasso the hearts of their very own cowboys! Only from

 and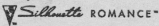

DOT